CW00347296

Be.

Harry Lawrence

CARTER/CARTIER

BY

H.P. LAWRENCE

Spinetinglers
PUBLISHING

Carter/Cartier
By H.P. Lawrence

First published 2013 by Spinetinglers Publishing

Spinetinglers Publishing
22 Vestry Road
Co. Down
BT23 6HJ
UK
www.spinetinglerspublishing.com

ISBN 978-1-906755-70-6

Printed in the UK.

This book is dedicated to the Isle of Wight
Heart Care and Rehabilitation Club.

CHAPTER 1

The Royal Navy Volunteer Reserve unit on the channel Island of Jersey were busy organising and packing all the equipment and paperwork the unit possessed. With the outbreak of war, and the rapid advance of the German army, Jersey and the other Channel Islands were preparing for the worst.

The RNVR unit had been ordered to England with everything they had, together with the unit's members and families that wished to go.

Lt. Commander Henry Carter, the unit's Commanding Officer was overseeing all the work. His two sons Roger and Richard and the rest of the unit were loading the old wooden ex-deep sea trawler, the unit's patrol craft, which had been fitted with the navy's latest equipment: including a forward 2″ gun and two mounted bren guns on the bridge, and one in the stern.

Most of the crew's families who were going to England had packed just enough food for the journey, the rest was given to friends and neighbours, who said they would look after the houses as best they could.

At 0800hrs on a wet May morning in 1941, Lt. Commander Henry Carter RNVR took his position on the bridge of HMS Flyby. "Cast off Roger, let's get going, I'll radio the harbourmaster and wish him well. Let go head rope, 20 starboard wheel, engage astern, stop engines, let go stern rope, slow ahead."

Roger waited until clear of other fishing boats before giving the order to stow fenders and secure ropes, which was done in a well organised routine.

"Right Addie," talking to the navigator, "course for Plymouth please."

Roger had been told that just before getting to the mine field an escort vessel would see them in. Two hours out of Jersey a shout from the stern lookout. "Aircraft astern, man the guns!" shouted Henry. "I've got the con."

Richard took his position at the forward 2in gun with a young able seaman, Vince Day and the cox'n took over the wheel. Roger headed for the stern gun, which was his position in case the bridge was knocked out.

Two seaman looked after the bridge bren guns, the engineers standing by their stations, all this took a matter of seconds.

"Any idea what sort of plane it is?" yelled Henry

"Zig zag course helmsman," Jake, the oldest member of the crew, replied to the affirmative. Jake had served on many great ships, and was now a very useful member of the unit.

The aircraft started a run along the port side of HMS FLYBY, it was a German spotter plane, and for sure was reporting the boats position right now.

"If it passes again all guns open fire," Harry remarked, turning to the engineer, "make sure everyone below is aware of what is going on."

"Aircraft approaching starboard side, looks like an attack run!" shouted the stern bren gunner.

"Turn to port helmsman get side on so all guns can come into play, when in range all guns open fire, raise the ensign Roger let him know we are ready for a fight."

Within two minutes, it was all over. The aircraft had

made it's run and started firing, but left it too late, missing the boat altogether, that was all HMS Flyby needed, with all guns blazing as the aircraft tried to turn away it was hit and rolled into a dive before plunging into the sea.

"Secure guns, helmsman alter course to original and lets get out of the area before any more come looking for us, navigator make sure the incident is logged, position etc."

The rest of the journey passed without any more incidents.

"Minefield starts about five miles ahead, should see our escort vessel soon," said the navigator.

Roger shouted to all hands to keep a lookout for the escort vessel and for any stray mines.

Henry Carter stood at his position on the bridge and thought how well his crew had acted against the plane, he felt quite proud that they could enter Plymouth with HMS Flyby's first kill.

Following the escort vessel they were taken to a pontoon which was occupied by MTBs and MGBs.

"Nice looking boats," Roger remarked to Richard.

"Be nice to have one," replied Richard.

"Secure the boat Roger, while I report to HQ," Henry

said putting on his jacket and cap. "Don't know how long I'll be, see that the crew and passengers get something hot and find out what's happening."

"Yes sir," replied Roger. "Brew up time cox'n, make the guest comfortable."

The navigator finished writing up the log just as a signal came through. "Signal from HQ Roger - All personal aboard HMS Flyby report to building N4."

"OK let's get going, it's getting late and I'm sure people are tired."

***

"Welcome to Plymouth Lt. Commander Carter, my name is Commodore Eric Knight. Glad you got here alright, I understand you had a little distraction?"

"Just a little sir, and thank you," answered Carter.

"Tonight we have good accommodation for yourself and crew, the families are being taken care of right now, they are going to a new block, just finished, until things are sorted. You go and rest I'll see you at o8oohrs tomorrow, and bring your officers with you," the Commodore said shaking Carter's hand.

"Thank you sir, and goodnight."

CHAPTER 2

Lt.Commander Henry Carter, together with his two sons, Roger and Richard, entered the officer's block to be greeted by a smiling Wren.

"Good morning sir, Commodore Knight is expecting you," she said showing them into the office.

Richard looked at Roger. "Nice one."

"Very," replied Roger.

Commodore Knight was standing by the window looking out on his charges. "What do you think, do you fancy training for command of one of those?" he asked Roger and Richard.

They both agreed. "We were hoping for something like that," Roger answered.

"Good, if you would both see Helen at the desk outside she has all the paperwork and instructions."

Roger and Richard Carter soon had everything that was required, and were told to report to block OF.2 for accommodation and to meet the instructors.

Meanwhile Henry Carter found himself being interviewed by four senior officers.

"So Lt.Com. if you were to look out of the window, how long would it take you to draw and paint what you see?" asked Captain Matthews.

Henry wondered why they were interested in his artwork. "Probably about two hours for a rough copy, maybe six hours for a good one. What's this all about? You know I have an art gallery in Jersey and two in France?"

Commodore Knight began to explain. "What we would like you to do, if you agree, is to take up residence in your Fécamp shop, you will be classed as a British agent working for naval intelligence. You would fit in well, you know the locals and speak French."

"What am I supposed to do there?" Henry asked, looking a little concerned.

Another Captain laid a map of Fécamp and the surrounding area on the desk. "Your shop is here, what do you see looking out of your window towards the harbour?"

"My shop is well positioned on the promenade and has extended views of most of the harbour."

"Exactly, we would like you to sketch and paint what you see: ships, troops, what uniforms they are wearing, most important we would then know what type of troops are around that area, also gun emplacements etc. Whatever you see paint it."

"Won't that look a little suspicious?" Henry asked.

Commodore Knight stood again by the window. "German officers like to pose, particularly away from home, makes them look important. We suggest you start by painting a German officer with the harbour as a back drop, they would like that to show off their authority, do a good painting for them and a rough copy for us."

"How would I send you the paintings?" queried Henry.

"You put the paintings and any other information into these waterproof tubes, then place them inside a fisherman's marker buoy, use an old one, put *No4* on it, take it along the coast to the little cove with a large rock."

"I know that place very well, I used to do fishing there," Henry said.

"Yes we know, that's why we thought it the best place. When there, put a weight on the buoy and throw it as near as possible to the left hand side of the rock it will be picked up by a frogman."

Henry asked how often it would be picked up and was told that no special arrangements were in place. "Every time the boats go over that way it will be done. Any problems you should move location and try and let us know."

The Captain with the charts made a suggestion that he started collecting washed up and old buoys to use in his paintings. "That way the Germans would be used to you walking around with marker buoys."

"I suppose it could work," muttered Henry.

"We will go over the final details after you have gone through some training: concealment, shaking off anyone following, small arms, and what signals we would use."

A Captain who had been standing listening asked if he thought any locals would betray him.

"Hard to say, I know most of them very well, we have always got on fine. New ones might just think I've came from another shop," Henry answered.

"OK that's settled; tomorrow you begin a week's training, sorry if it sounds a short time but we want this in place quickly, things are happening in France very fast and the sooner we know what the better," Commodore Knight said as he gathered up the charts and paperwork.

"After your week we will meet back here for any final problems etc. Thank you very much gentlemen, and thank you Lt. Commander Carter for your co-operation in this."

CHAPTER 3

Lt. Roger Carter was assigned to No3 training section, which was a motor torpedo flotilla.

Lt. Richard Carter joined No5 training section, a motor gun boat flotilla.

They were both very excited and looked forward to training and their first patrol. Just six days into their training all training officers were called to the Op's room.

"Please sit gentlemen," said Commander Wears. "We have just received information that a large German convoy is expected coming down the channel close to the French coast, picking up ammunition and fuel at Le Harve, heading for north Africa, it will be well escorted plenty of E-boats and patrol vessels."

There was a few 'wows' and 'oh boys' as Commander Wears drew the possible course.

"Right settle down, what this means is that we will have to put every boat to sea. Boat allocations have been made up and are on the table at the back, orders are on the boats now, please report to your boats and good luck."

***

Roger Carter made his way along the pontoon, passing three other MTBs before reaching MTB 147.

Lt. Leonard Murrey welcomed him with a broad smile. "Welcome aboard Roger, come below and get sorted. This is PO Stephen Tasker, he's cox'n and keeps the crew on their toes. Cox'n this is Lt. Roger Carter second in command, show him around, get him up to speed with as much as possible. We sail at 2100hrs, I'll be at the chart table."

For Roger Carter it was a whirlwind tour of the boat, trying to take it all in.

"You'll get used to things very quickly it's not a big boat, we are always in each other's way, officers get priority," said Tasker.

"How's the rest of the crew?" asked Roger.

"A good crew; we have a new forward gunner this trip, previous one got promotion and is now a training PO."

Roger made his way to the chart room.

"Taken it all in?" asked the skipper.

"Got some of it, expect it will come easy enough," replied Roger.

"Very quickly," said Leonard Murrey. "When we sail take the navigation until I call all hands to stations, then look after the stern gun with Matthew, he's experienced. You know the drill anything happens to me you take over, a good crew, they will help you, now let's hope we have a good trip."

Roger stowed his gear then made himself known to the rest of the crew, again checking the fire appliances and ammunition lockers.

"Call all hands for sandwiches and tea," Leonard told the cox'n. "After that single up and await the off."

***

Six MTBs and four gun boats left Plymouth silently, only being watched by maintenance and dock workers, wondering how many would return; they were used to this.

"Signal from lead boat sir," said Harry, the bridge gunner and medical orderly. "All boats single file until clear of minefield, follow escort boat."

"Acknowledge," remarked the skipper.

Once clear of the minefield the flotilla split into two lines: MTBs in one, gun boats in the other.

Darkness was closing in, the lead boat signalled to slow ahead to save on fuel and make less wake, which at night could often be seen cruising along at 6kts. With no lights everyone soon got night vision.

Now the waiting game began.

Two hours passed, it was 11:40 p.m. The lead boat signalled convoy sighted 10deg port bow, MTBs fan out to starboard, gun boats to port.

"Crew to stations!" shouted Murrey.

"Cox'n on the wheel," Tasker replied.

"No1 in position," answered Roger.

Soon all boats could see the escorts, fast E-boats coming towards them.

"Prepare for attack, fire when in range, I'll try and pick

out a target!" yelled Murrey.

The gun boats had already started firing, followed almost instantly by the MTBs.

The lead boat sent up two flares, which lit up the darkness.

Out of the smoke came a row of E-boats all firing, the MTB nearest the lead boat suddenly exploded just after releasing two torpedoes.

The firing became more intent as all boats passed each other, the torpedoes from the sinking MTB found their way to a small freighter which exploded and started listing to starboard.

"Target ahead!" shouted Murrey. "Large freighter well down in the water, stand by torpedoes!"

Just as he was about to say fire, a stream of tracer bullets raced across the bridge killing Murrey and the port bridge gunner instantly.

Roger, on seeing this, moved quickly to the bridge, looked at Murrey then at the fallen gunner, turning to the cox'n who was bleeding from the shoulder and said, "you alright?"

"I'll be fine, last order was large freighter ahead

torpedoes ready to fire sir."

"Fire torpedoes," he told the seaman in charge, "then turn to port cox'n."

"It's all yours now sir," said Tasker the cox'n.

A loud boom sound came from the freighter as the two torpedoes hit below the water line, followed by the sound of metal against metal.

"Some heavy machines on that one," said the cox'n.

A big explosion lit up the night sky as the freighter began to roll.

"Watch out E-Boat closing starboard side!" yelled the forward gunner as he opened fire. The rear gunner also opened fire hitting the E-Boat's bridge, the vessel must have lost control; it turned to starboard then stopped.

"If it fires finish it off, if not leave it, it will sink soon enough," Roger said as he turned towards the convoy. "Let's make a last quick pass, we should have enough ammunition, see what we can do, the others look OK, just keep a good lookout".

Another freighter burst into flames followed by a small coaster.

"Make for the large trawler!" Roger shouted. "She looks

well down."

With all guns firing at the trawler, which put out little response, it soon began to blasé.

"I think we have company from seaward!" yelled the rear gunner. "Can't make out what but moving fast."

"Hard to port cox'n make for the rest of the flotilla."

Another small coaster burst into flames and began to lean over. "E-Boats retreating, new arrivals; MTBs, looks like the Falmouth flotilla," said the cox'n.

"Signal sir, well done, we will take over now. Safe journey home."

"Acknowledge, let's make for home follow the rest, and look out for anyone in the water, forward gunner take over the wheel, give the cox'n a break."

Getting the two dead bodies under cover Roger turned to the crew, "Well done all, the skipper told me I could rely on you, once again well done."

On the way back Roger counted the boats: two MTBs missing and one gun boat.

The cox'n came on the bridge. "Hot drink sir and well done to you. There's a little something in it, the skipper always liked something on the way home."

"Thanks cox'n," Roger said. "So this is what MTBs are all about…"

CHAPTER 4

Lt. Richard Carter was called to Commodore Knight's office just after 3 p.m.

"Ah Lt. Carter, a little job for you tonight," turning to a chart on his desk. "You will be dropping an agent as close as possible to this little inlet here," he said, pointing with his finger.

"I know that place very well; Dad would often take Roger and myself fishing there."

There was a knock on the door. "Enter," said Commodore Knight.

Richard looked up with a surprise as his father entered the office.

"Hello Richard, I'm your passenger for tonight, Commodore Knight has let me use his office to explain."

Moving over to the chart Henry Carter began to tell what

he was going to do. "It will be nice to see some old friends again," Henry continued, telling Richard that he would be sinking an old marker buoy or something similar between the big rock in the centre of the little inlet and the shore to the west.

Richard said he was worried as that part of the French coast was full of Germans.

Commodore Knight tapped on the door and entered. "I've been called away, so I'll say my goodbye and good luck, it's going to be an overcast night so should make for an easy trip."

Left alone Henry explained he would be using his French name, Henri Cartier, and said how sorry he was that he was able to see Roger before he left.

***

2300hrs on an overcast night, with rain showers making for a wet crossing, the small gunboat slipped her lines and followed the escort vessel through the mine field.

"Make direct for Fécamp, we will change heading nearer the other side," said Richard to his No1.

0300hrs the gun boat eased to a stop, two seaman had gotten the fold up canoe over the side holding the ropes while Henry Carter said his goodbye.

"Good luck Father, take care and regards to all at the shop," Richard said as his father vanished into the night.

"Let's get home cox'n. Lookouts, keep a good watch."

***

Meanwhile Roger Carter was nearing Plymouth.

"Escort vessel sighted skipper," reported the starboard lookout.

"Follow the others in helmsman," Roger answered.

The journey back from the encounter with the convoy had been slow, some of the boats were damaged, the lead boat gave orders to stay together.

Roger eased the MTB alongside, where ambulance staff were waiting; a routine which happened every time the boats come back.

"Once we have unloaded I'll report in, get the skipper and seaman Holmes' gear packed ready for collection."

The cox'n knew the drill, he had been there before.

Roger made direct to the Op's room, where he was told Commodore Knight was waiting.

"Sorry about Lt. Murrey, a good man, you certainly were put to the test," said the Commodore

"The cox'n is putting his belongings together, along with seaman Holmes, another good man," Roger answered.

"The maintenance crew will get on with any repairs as soon as your crew have finished. We have to keep going."

A knock on the door broke the atmosphere.

"Some good news sir, reports just came in; only two ships undamaged, five ships sunk, rest returned to Le-Havre. Three E-boats destroyed, Falmouth MTBs lost one boat, they thanked the Plymouth boats for doing most of the work, well done, end of signal."

"I suppose on that note we should call it a success," remarked Commodore Knight.

"One convoy less to worry about," answered Roger.

"Take tomorrow off, report back here 0800hrs day after, some changes happening."

Roger headed for MTB147 to collect his gear, where the cox'n greeted him. The bodies had been removed with their belongings. The crew had been dismissed and returned to barracks until the boat had been repaired.

"And what about you?" Roger asked.

"Oh I have a lady friend waiting," said Tasker.

"Well take care, maybe we will sail together again." Roger said as he made his way below to have a look around and collect his own belongings, before going to the officer's mess.

**

Richard Carter woke Roger at 0730hrs the next morning, he explained what had happened and how he had taken their father over and what he was going to do.

"He said he was sorry he could not say goodbye but the tides were just right and a good overcast night, he wished us both well and hoped to see us soon."

CHAPTER 5

Henri walked into his shop at 17 Rue Prom, Fécamp.

"Can I help you sir? Oh goodness it's you! What are you doing here? The place is crawling with Germans," said the startled Pierre an old and trusted friend of Henri and his boys.

"I'm staying here for a while, doing some paintings."

"Knowing you there will be something else," Pierre said.

"If I don't tell you, you won't know, safer that way. I'll get myself organised first then tell you everything."

"I'll get the upstairs room ready for you, it's in a mess just been used for storage. I still live at home, my wife Val died last year, I had no way of letting you know."

"How's things been?" asked Henri.

"Not too bad for most, but they are ruthless with some. There is a strict curfew on, nobody out after 8 p.m."

They both went upstairs and soon made light work of clearing the room. Pierre said he would get some clean bed linen from his house and some food to keep Henri going until he had time to shop.

Twenty minutes later Pierre was back in the shop. "A bottle of red, and bread with some nice cheese."

Henri and Pierre spent that evening talking over old times.

Henri told how his sons were doing, and asked Pierre if the cove where he used to fish with his sons was still the same.

"Still the same old rocky path, nobody goes there anymore, not since the Germans blocked it off. Why the interest? What you up to?" Pierre asked with a look over the top of his glasses.

"How would I get to the big rock in the mouth of the cove?"

He was told the only way was through the gap between the twin rocks at low tide.

"How about the locals, do you think they would say anything about who I am?"

"The ones that know you would be alright, the others

would just think you have always been here. I'll make sure the locals know you will be staying."

Henri said goodnight and would see him in the morning. He fell asleep easily, but was awoken at 0630hrs by the sound of banging and drilling.

He looked out of the window and could see plenty of activity at one of the berths; a large cargo vessel was being unloaded. He noticed armoured personal carriers, troop carriers, ammunition and other stores.

Henri made a note of all he could see, before going to the rear of the shop looking for any old marker buoys, having no luck he went into the back yard where he found an old crab pot marker, *a little small* he thought.

He took it back into the shop, fitted a tube into it, then put the list he had done, adding the name of the ship into the buoy. Henri gathered his drawing pad and pencils and waited for Pierre to arrive, before going to check out the cove.

Pierre told Henri to be careful as many Germans were around and were always asking for papers, and if they found a painting in a buoy he would be taken to HQ, and probably shot.

As he strolled along the road leading to the cove he took note of all he saw, thinking he would write it all down as soon as he got back to the shop.

Stopping at a junction to let a convoy pass, he took mental notes of what vehicles they were, when a voice behind him made him jump. "Are you crazy, what are you doing here?"

Startled, Henri turned to see Ramond Le'tore, the local police sergeant.

"Ramond, how are you? I've moved into my shop at Rue Prom to do some painting."

"I don't know anything, so keep your head down, some nasty people about, keep well aware of anybody that may be watching you."

"Thank you Ramond, see you around. If anyone should ask you might say I'm often there, moving between here and my Paris shop."

"Take care Henri," said Ramond as he continued on his way.

Henri headed for some woods, out of sight of the road and the footpath which lead to the little cove. He made his way slowly through the woods until he was opposite the old broken down gate, checking all was clear he started down the rocky pathway, through some wire and a wooden barrier before reaching the shoreline.

Getting onto the beach he found himself some cover among some rocks, made a few extra notes and put them into the marker buoy.

Henri waited for about ten minutes, checking if all was still clear. He rolled up his trousers, took off his shoes then heaved the buoy with its weight close to the big rock, knowing that it will be covered by the tide in about three hours.

Henri climbed back to the top, pulling out his sketchpad he began drawing the rocky cove. After a short while the sound of a vehicle coming towards him. *No sudden movement*, he thought as the car stopped.

"Good day, what may I ask are you doing out here?" said the young German officer.

"Painting the scenery, I'm an artist I have a shop in town, are you interested in portrait painting?" answered Henri.

"Have you got your papers?"

"Yes here," said Henri handing the officer his papers.

"I suggest you get back to your shop, curfew starts in an

hour."

"Could I come here again, as painting is my only income? Maybe you could tell other officers that I do portraits with a nice scenery background; my other shop in Paris is very popular."

The young officer thought for a while. "I will come to your shop tomorrow and see your work, now time to leave, good day to you."

Henri walked back to town, as he approached his shop he saw the German officer coming out, he stopped outside and looked at the paintings in the window. Henri hung back standing in a doorway watching. Soon the officer walked off and Henri went straight into the shop.

"What did that German officer want?" he asked.

"He just looked at some paintings and said he would be back tomorrow. I told him we are trying to rearrange the shop and more paintings will be on display soon."

"Good, I met him up near the cove, he said he will ask if any officers might like a portrait."

Pierre made coffee and asked Henri if he had eaten, producing some bread and sausage. "I must get to the shops tomorrow, and get recognised," Henri said as Pierre left.

That evening Henri started drawing what he could see from the upstairs window - a good view of the harbour.

CHAPTER 6

Lt. Roger Carter entered the Commodore's office, it had been raining hard and he was glad of a few minutes of comfort.

"Good morning sir," Roger said as he was gestured to a chair.

"MTB 147 will take quite a time to fix, plus we are putting some new gear on her."

Roger looked concerned, what was coming next?

"We have a position for you at Chatham, commanding MTB 265, interested?"

"Yes sir, sounds great to me," Roger replied with a smile on his face. "Thank you sir."

"You will take command day after tomorrow, all the details and your paperwork pick up from admin, and good luck."

The Commodore shook hands and said that he would pass on any news regarding his father.

That evening Roger and Richard sat talking about their father. "At least he knows his way about," said Richard.

"Wish him well from me," replied Roger.

"I must go now Roger, take care of yourself, the flotilla leaves at 2200hrs," Richard remarked giving Roger a big hug.

Roger started packing for his trip to Chatham, thinking about his father, knowing how times had changed.

***

Henri Cartier opened the shop at 0900hrs, got a bucket of water and cloth, and started cleaning the front windows and door.

Got to be seen doing normal jobs he thought to himself. Henri noticed the bakers shop just three doors away was open.

"Good morning Robir," Henri said. "Nice to see you again."

"Good morning Henri," replied Robir. "Come in, what

are you doing back at this time? Ramond Le'tore told me last night you were here, he said if I see you to tell you to act normal."

They talked for a while, Henri said his sons were doing fine and he hoped to do some painting while there. Henri had just finished cleaning when a staff car pulled up outside the shop. Two uniformed German officers got out and started looking at the paintings in the window.

Henri opened the door. "Would you like to see more inside gentlemen? I specialise in portraits."

The two officers entered, after a short while one asked if Henri could do a portrait of him with a nice background.

"Of cause, what type of background would you like? Do you want a background of your work place, or your HQ, or maybe just a dockland view?"

Henri thought *am I pushing it too far?*

"I am a transport commander, a background with plenty of trucks in it would do nicely."

"That should look very nice, it would show your authority. How big a picture would you expect?"

"About 60x40cm; quite big. I have a large fireplace with plenty of space above back in Germany, it will look nice;

when can you start?"

"I'll do the background first, so if you could get me into the motor pool for say two days that will be enough, the portrait we can do here anytime".

"Very good, I'll let you know when, thank you and good day to you."

The two officers left, leaving Henri with a big grin, this was just what he wanted.

Henri began getting his canvas and paints ready in the back room, his sketch book and ample pencils were put into his artists bag along with some water colour paints to get the colour of uniforms and any insignias on the vehicles that might give a clue to which unit's were there. He would use the sketch pad to do a rough copy, with as much detail as possible, then copy what he thought the subject would be happy with onto the big canvas: the copy he would touch up and send to England.

After having a light lunch with Robir the baker, talking over old times and assuring him everything was alright, Henri decided to put the first primer coat on the canvas when Pierre called, "come and see this!" He sounded excited.

Henri stood outside his shops door watching as a big supply ship came limping into the docks, with the aid of two tugs.

There was a lot of activity, trucks and troops heading for the dock gates.

Pierre turned to Henri. "Someone has had a busy time, looks quite damaged"

Henri muttered "pity it didn't sink."

Getting back into the shop Henri began drawing a sketch of the scene, including the vessel's name, *another one for England* he thought.

The rest of the day was spent taking notes of what was being unloaded.

Next morning Pierre came into the shop with a smile on his face. "You know that old crane on jetty 4? It broke while lifting a big crate of ammunition from that ship that's damaged, it fell into the water."

"That will delay things a little," Henri said looking out of the window. "I'll make some coffee, then I want to have a look around."

***

Two days passed before Henri was contacted, he had meanwhile been busy sketching the harbour scenes.

"Good day, would you come to the motor pool and see what you and the commandant would like as a background? We have a staff car waiting," said the younger German corporal looking all around the shop watching Pierre as he sorted some paperwork.

"Yes I'll get my gear," Henri said as he went to the back room, telling Pierre where he was going, and to expect him back in about four hours.

The gates to the compound were well guarded, the corporal signed Henri in before going to the office block.

"Glad you were able to come today, we will be very busy for the next few days, so I hope you can sort out a good background."

"Once we find a good setting I'll be about four hours, I can finish the finer details back in my shop, then all that remains is for you to come for your portrait." Looking around Henri noticed a row of vehicles. "Maybe all those different types of vehicles with those sheds behind, and once you are placed in the foreground it gives the painting a vision of what you are in charge of?"

"Yes good idea; corporal, get some more vehicles out, and help Cartier with any more he requires. I must be off now plenty to do, the corporal will see you home when you have done. Good day Cartier."

Henri settled himself in a sheltered position where he had a clear view of most of the motor pool, he soon noticed at least four different types of uniform.

After a short time sketching the trucks and buildings, paying attention to all the markings, he started on the uniforms; some were Afrika Korps, some were infantry, others he had no idea of, but thought London would know. He continued looking for any other information that might be of interest.

"Ready when you are corporal," Henri said packing his gear away. "I might have to come back again, but not for a few days."

Approaching the gates they had to stop; a convoy of trucks laden with sailors were coming into the compound. *Probably from the damaged ship*, Henri thought. "Thank you corporal," he said getting out of the car.

Robir was watching. "What you been up to?" he asked.

"Just some painting, tell you one day," Henri remarked with a smile.

"You be very careful, people will talk," answered Robir.

Henri sorted his painting gear and sketch book onto the table in the back of the shop.

"How did it go?" asked Pierre.

"Very well I think, got something to get started on."

Pierre had made some stew. "You must eat."

"I'll go and look around tomorrow and get some food."

Henri slept well that night, the noise from the docks didn't worry him.

He woke at 0600hrs and looked out the window; the docks were busy, they must have worked all night. There were trucks everywhere waiting to load, the damaged vessel was high in the water now and listing to port, exposing a large hole just below the bridge.

Pierre came in at 0930hrs, bringing some bread and cheese. "Now if you are going shopping keep to the main street, it's busier there, nobody takes any notice."

"I thought after I might go to the old fishing quarter and look for some old fenders, they add to the background in the paintings."

"Don't go too near the big boats, they are manned by the Germans for coastal work," explained Pierre.

Henri walked around the shops, noticing how short of stock they all looked. Getting himself some basic supplies he headed for the fishing jetty.

"Good morning," he said to a young man sitting on a small fishing boat, packed with nets, lobster pots and other fishing gear.

The fisherman eyed Henri, looking at him with suspicion. "Good morning," the young man replied.

"Is this your boat? I'm looking for any old fenders and old buoys."

"Come aboard, I think I might be able to help you, I have two old marker buoys you can have, can't use them now, not allowed to drop any pots over the side; things are very limited these days".

Henri thanked him saying he needed them to use as a background for his paintings.

"You that man who has the art shop in Rue Prom?"

"Yes that's me," answered Henri.

"Things are noticed around here, you have only just come and seem very friendly with the Germans."

Henri thought for a while. *How do I answer that, I'll take a chance, is there anyone I could talk to and explain.*

"People might wonder which side you on, they could be wary."

Henri asked if the fisherman knew Pierre who runs the art shop, or Ramond Le'tore the local police sergeant.

"I know Le'tore and Pierre. Come and see me about 6 p.m., I'll have a couple of marker buoys for you."

Henri thanked the young fisherman, saying he would be back later.

On the way to his shop he took note of the uniforms that he saw, paying attention to the insignias.

Entering the shop Henri was met by Pierre.

"I found a young fisherman, he said to call back later; he has some marker buoys for me. He knows I've not been here long, he is worried because I've been seen with the Germans".

"Henri sit down, let's talk, I think I know you well enough." Pierre got two glasses and a bottle of wine from under the counter. "Henri you have heard of small pockets of resistance? Well there is one here, so they have to be very careful who they speak to, before I tell you more I *must* know why you are here."

Henri pondered for a few moments. "Pierre I am here to gather what information I can on activities, what type of troops are around here, and equipment."

Pierre said he guessed something like that. "But why the interest in the little cove?"

"That will be how I get the information back to England, the paintings all have a background," he said opening his folder of the motor pool. "You see Pierre all the types of trucks and their markings, and other types of vehicles, note the uniforms, all tell a story. I'll put copies of what I paint in the marker buoys, and hopefully sell the originals. I then take the buoy to the little cove where it will be picked up, weather permitting quite often. That's why I am keeping the Germans happy."

"Thank you Henri, you go and see the young fisherman this evening, remember curfew is at 8 p.m."

They talked for a while then finished the wine before Pierre left.

Henri sat for awhile wondering if all was going to plan, had he given too much information? *No*, he thought, *I've known Pierre a long time.*

At 5:30 p.m. Pierre arrived back at the shop. "I'm coming with you, there's someone who would like to see you."

"What's this all about?" Henri asked.

"Let's get going, it's the best time of day, plenty of people leaving work."

The young fisherman was waiting by his boat. "Follow me, we are going to a house around the corner."

Henri and Pierre followed and were soon inside a small terraced house where they were told to wait in the lounge.

The door opened and in came six men followed by Sgt. Ramond Le'Tore.

"Henri, how are you?" Ramond asked. "There are a few questions we would liked answered, namely what you are doing back here at this time, and why so friendly with the Germans?"

Henri thought for a while. "Before I answer I would like to ask Pierre a question," he said. "Pierre would you trust these people with your life?"

Pierre replied straight away. "Of course, I would not have bought you here otherwise."

"That will do for me," Henri said and began telling them why he was at Fécamp and why he needed marker buoys.

After a while Ramond said, "you must understand our position, Pierre is our leaflet printer among other things, now let's have a glass of wine before curfew."

Henri was introduced to the others who wished him well.

"I might be able to give you some pictures of the inner docks, as last week we had an accident and I took some photos before the Germans took over," Ramond explained.

Pierre told everyone they should leave two at a time.

Henri was given two marker buoys, he thanked them all saying they knew where he was if he could help.

Slinging the buoys over his shoulder he strolled direct to his shop.

Henri slept well that night, thinking at least he had some friends.

CHAPTER 7

Lt. Roger Carter had arrived at Chatham dockyards. He reported to the admin office where he was told he was to take command of MTB 265. The admin staff introduced him to his No1, a young Sub. Lt. called Junior, as he had the same name as the commanding officer.

"I'll introduce you to the crew, a really good bunch," Junior said as they headed for MTB265.

Roger stood for a moment looking over the railings at his boat. "A nice looking vessel No1."

"A very nice boat sir," replied Junior.

Roger was told the crew were well trained, the Cox,n said he would give him a tour of the boat.

"A good boat sir, rides well." the cox'n said. "This is your cabin, a bit small I'm afraid sir."

"Not to worry cox'n, I'm used to small boats, anyway I

don't expect I'll be using it much. Thanks for the tour."

Junior shouted, "Skipper to the bridge!"

Roger arrived to find junior looking for his cap. "What's up No1?" Roger asked.

"Brass coming along the jetty sir."

"Right cox'n look busy, men below."

"Good morning Lt.," said Captain Jones, "this is Lt. Com Slater, your flotilla leader, sorry he did not see you when you arrived yesterday, he's had a spot of leave." Right I'll leave you two to get on, I'm off to some meeting."

"Welcome to Chatham Roger, we are a busy unit, always plenty to do."

***

Henri was just finishing his first picture of the motor pool when Pierre came in with a bowl of soup.

"You must eat or you will lose your strength, which you may need," Pierre said putting the soup on the table.

"I forgot the time, I've been working most of the night."

Pierre looked at the painting. "I can see why the English wish you to do this, so much detail of the motor pool and uniforms, very good Henri."

"When the painting is dry I must get it to the cove, I must be there before the high tide."

A little later Henri rolled the painting and placed it into a waterproof tube then into the marker buoy, taking care it could not be seen.

Picking up two other buoys and a length of rope he headed for the little cove. Once outside the town he kept to the wooded area, finally reaching the cove he had a good look around before making his way down the narrow path which ended at the beach near the big rock.

Waiting for a few moments, to make sure he was not followed, Henri tied the marker buoy to a small rock just near the big one. He checked the area where he had put a buoy two days ago; he could not find it. *Must have been picked up* he thought.

Henri headed back to town and turned the corner near his shop; he stopped suddenly, in front was a check point barrier across the road.

"Papers," said a young German corporal. "What are those?" he asked, pointing to the two marker buoys slug over Henri's shoulder.

"These are marker buoys to add to the scenery in the painting of the commandant of the motor pool," Henri said looking at the German corporal, "it makes the painting look natural."

The young German quickly looked at Henri's papers. "Carry on," he said nervously.

Once in the shop he asked Pierre what was going on.

"There was an incident at the docks, someone tried to steal food from the German food store, they are looking for him now. How did things go at the cove?"

"It went fine, I'll need a steady supply of buoys though," said Henri making his way to the back room. "I must get on with the original painting."

"I'll see what I can get at the fisherman's quarter," Pierre answered as he left Henri to his work.

CHAPTER 8

Lt. Richard Carter was about half-way across the English Channel. "Slow to 8knt," he told the cox'n, "we don't want to make too much bow wave, not on a still night like this."

After another forty minutes the port lookout muttered in a quiet sound "something port quarter."

Richard grabbed his binoculars. "Looks like a Sub, can't quite make it out, too low in the water. Stop engines, lets hang around until it passes, probably going to Brest, keep a good eye on her lookouts."

Richard had left Plymouth alone, he had been told his MGB was one of the fastest, also he might like the job of picking up the marker buoys from the cove as he had often been there and knew it well.

The submarine passed without any problems, Richard thought *now is the time he would have liked an MTB*.

"Half ahead cox'n, continue on original heading."

Seaman Darby the bridge gunner, was also the boat's frogman, and it was his job to collect the marker buoys.

"Nice night for a paddle," Richard said as Darby came onto the bridge.

"Just go over the details again sir."

"All going well I'll drop you as close as I can off the cove entrance, once we can see the big rock, you head for the right hand side of the rock, as you get level with it turn right, the marker buoy should be somewhere there tied to the bottom somehow."

"Lights on the starboard bow skipper," whispered the lookout.

"Entrance to Fécamp," Richard answered, "port five."

"Port five," answered the cox'n, "five port wheel on."

"Head for the big rock, there, slow ahead."

"Get ready Darby ten minutes," Richard said checking that all was clear ahead. "Lookouts keep a good eye on any movement."

It took only two minutes to get the fold up canoe ready.

"Over you go Darby, we will wait here as long as possible. If I have to move off I'll be back in two hours, don't get caught with the marker buoy; good luck."

Seaman Darby slipped into the canoe and headed for the big rock, the tide was with him, just coming up to high water. The big rock looked even bigger up close, once level he turned right, the visibility was almost zero, when suddenly he bumped into the marker buoy, Darby quickly untied it from its weight, putting it safely into the canoe he headed back to the MGB.

Richard had told the crew to keep quiet and to listen for the canoe or any other sounds.

After about twenty five minutes a little noise was heard. "Canoe on port side" whispered the lookout.

"Get him aboard as quick as possible, cox'n get ready, let's move out quietly. Gun crews keep a good look out."

Seaman Darby gave Richard the marker buoy, saying it would be easier if he could arrive half hour later just as the tide was turning, as it was hard going on the way back and the entrance to the cove when the tide is still coming in gets quite rough.

"Noted Darby, will put that on the chart."

Richard put the marker buoy into a sack which was tied to a weight, telling the cox'n and Darby that if anything was to happen on the way back to throw it overboard. "It must not be found by the Germans."

"Right cox'n I think we are clear, let her rip."

After a couple of hours of everyone being on their toes it came as a welcome sound when the forward gunner shouted "Plymouth escort vessel sighted sir!"

"Signal her that we are coming home," answered Richard.

Once alongside the pontoon, Richard told the cox'n to secure the boat while he took the marker buoy to the CO's office, where Commodore Knight was waiting.

"Everything go alright Richard? Let's have a look at the painting." Removing the tube from the buoy and taking out the rolled up painting, Commodore Knight placed it on his desk. "Well, Well," he said, "a lot of detail there, it looks like those vehicles are going to North Africa, quite a few different uniforms too. Better get this to HQ as soon as possible, well done."

Richard returned to his boat, which was being refuelled and armament checked; the crew had gone ashore for breakfast and some heads down.

PO Brady, who was controlling the refuelling remarked,

"Better get something to eat and have a rest sir, all boats going out tonight."

"Thank you PO, I'll do that."

Richard had breakfast, and soon fell asleep wondering how his father was doing.

***

Richard woke with a jump, sweating, he sat on his bunk, what a dream: family arguments, mother running off with a Frenchman, father in an occupied country, Roger moving to Chatham.

He looked at the time; two hours before dinner, time for a shower, after which he felt better.

Richard headed for his gun boat, meeting Ginger Gibbons, his No1, on the way.

"I hear we are all going out in force tonight skipper."

"Yes, that's why I'm going to the boat, to check her over."

"That's what I am doing," Ginger replied.

As they approached MGB824 Ginger noticed an extra gun had been placed on the bridge. "That will come in handy," he said.

"Very nice too," Richard remarked. "Let's see what else we have."

The MGB was fully fuelled and there was extra ammunition. "I see we have a box of sandwiches, looks like it could be a long night, do they know something we don't?" said Ginger.

"I suspect they do, just have to wait for the briefing."

***

Commodore Knight entered the operations room with a Royal marine major. "Please sit gentlemen, this is Major Matthews, who will explain one half of tonight's operation. Firstly this is for the MTB flotilla, a large convoy is expected coming into the channel from north Africa, destination unknown, the Falmouth unit along with our unit of MTBs and gun boats will attack, I expect it will be well supported by escort vessels, and once in the channel E-boats. The plan is to press an attack with torpedoes while the gun boats attack the escort vessels, this will continue until the convoy gets within range of Portsmouth unit, who will take over. Once past that point Shoreham and Newhaven units take over. We intend to hit this convoy hard, information is the convoy might be aiming for one of the French ports to load trucks, tanks, ammunition and supplies for north Africa."

Major Matthews stood up. "Gentlemen, two gun boats will be assigned to me, myself and twelve marines are going to raid a Chateau near the small town of Manour, we have information that a VIP from the free French, who can help organise the French in England, has been taken prisoner he is in the local police station, probably waiting to be moved."

Major Matthews then explained that six marines and three canoes would be on each boat, he then uncovered a chart on the wall of the area.

"I have been told the water is quite deep around the approach to Manour, so the MGBs should get fairly close to shore, but that's up to each skipper. Once the marines are on their way the MGBs can go back out to sea and wait for the signal to come close in to pick us up; the signal will be four short flashes repeated three times, the signal will be at ground level so we need sharp eyes. Once the signal has been sent the marines will start paddling out to you. Right gentlemen, that's all for now, the two MGBs are 824 and 228, paperwork for each is on the table at the back. Thank you gentlemen and good luck."

Richard and Ginger picked up their paperwork, and headed back to the boat.

"Get the crew together Ginger, briefing in fifteen minutes."

After explaining to the crew what was happening and what was expected, Richard told Ginger to organise the marines when they come aboard; he and the cox'n would be going over the approach to Manour.

"Marines coming aboard sir, with three canoes, very nice too, I'll get them stowed and secure!" Ginger yelled. "That means the marines as well," he said with a smile.

A voice from the bridge called, "signal sir, flotilla ready in fifteen minutes. Escort vessel taking up position now."

"Single up Ginger, you take her out while I have a word with the marines."

Richard sat in the small confines of the gun boats space below. "Welcome aboard, just a couple of points: if we are attacked I would appreciate help, if we have a fire the crew will deal with it unless we ask for help, and if we abandon ship use your canoes if possible, and good luck with your mission."

A burly sergeant said, "thank you and just make sure you are there to pick us up."

"Try my best, now let's get underway."

***

Back on the bridge Richard watched as the flotilla led by the escort vessel went through the port defences, once clear Richard told Ginger to follow the lead boat through the mine field, then the flotilla would turn to starboard until they meet up with the Falmouth flotilla at waypoint double 2.

"When we meet with the Falmouth boys we alter course to waypoint foxtrot, continue on that heading until flotilla leader tell us and 228 to continue with our mission."

The weather was overcast, slight to moderate sea.

"No rain yet," said the cox'n.

"I don't know if that's good or bad," Ginger replied, "for the marines I mean."

"Signal from 228 sir," said a lookout. "Ten minutes to drop."

"Right Ginger the boat's mine, get the marines ready."

The approach to Manour went without any incidents.

"This is as far as we can go Sergeant, it's up to you now. Good luck, we await your signal."

MGB228 was about forty feet off 824's port side, the canoes were being loaded two marines to each.

The canoes paddled silently towards the shore, and were soon out of site, the two MGBs turned seawards and moved slowly away.

"Everyone keep eyes and ears fully alert, we have a couple of hours hanging around."

"Searchlight port side heading this way," whispered a lookout".

"Checking the shoreline, everyone quiet, hope they don't pick up the canoes," Ginger said.

The small patrol craft moved slowly past, before moving out of site round a headland.

About an hour passed.

"There's the signal sir, four short repeated three times."

"Move inshore slowly, don't want to make noise or

wash, keep extra watch in case that patrol boat comes back."

"Canoes sighted starboard bow."

"Get hands ready to get them aboard quickly Ginger," Richard remarked. "Cox'n keep the boat steady."

"Welcome back Sergeant, let's get you all below," Ginger said as he counted all six marines back. "What about your VIP?"

"He's with Major Matthews in the other boat," said the sergeant.

The other MGB had already turned and was heading seaward when a star shell lit up the two MGBs.

"Patrol craft seen us and opened fire sir!" yelled the cox'n.

"Return fire, head towards her cox'n, let's draw her away from 228, give them chance to get going."

The gunboat was soon racing past the small patrol craft, and with all guns firing her wheelhouse was soon shattered, the patrol craft began losing way and stopped firing.

"Cease firing, leave her, head for home cox'n, Ginger take over I'm just below."

Richard asked the sergeant how things went.

"Very good, not much resistance, we only had two slight injuries and we got our man OK."

The journey back was straight forward, the escort vessel was waiting and soon the two MGBs were tied up alongside the pontoon, the marines left leaving the crews of MGB824 and 228 waiting for the return of the MTBs.

CHAPTER 9

Henri was busy painting in the back room when the shop door opened "Good day is Henri Cartier in?" the German officer asked Pierre.

Henri entered the shop front, closing the door behind him.

"Good morning to you, can I help you?"

"I am Captain Hienrich Mass, I met you just out of town, you were sketching."

"That's right I recognise you now," Henri answered.

"My superior would like a portrait, your work has been noted."

"I am doing one at the moment, but yes when he is ready," Henri answered thinking of another scene.

"My superior is the commandant at Cherbourg, you will have to go there, transport will be arranged."

"That's fine all work is welcome."

Hienrich Mass said he would let Henri know, in about two days time he expected.

Henri and Pierre agreed that the docks at Cherbourg should have some interesting activity.

"I'd better get this one finished and get it to the cove. I'll also say I have to go to Cherbourg for a couple of days."

"You be careful in Cherbourg, they don't know you there, but they can pick up a Jersey accent, not a lot of love between them," Pierre explained.

"I'll be careful, hopefully it will only take two days and I can finish most of the details back here."

***

Three days passed. Henri had gone to the cove, he had found another way through the wood which gave him more cover, he told Pierre he must allow more time as the tide was coming in fast and he had wet trousers and boots.

"If you were stopped like that the SS would be involved."

"I must hide some more clothes to change into, maybe in

the wood."

That evening Henri and Pierre were talking about all the good times they had been through, enjoying a glass of wine, when a knock on the door made them jump; it was Heinrich Mass.

"Sorry it's late, but would you leave for Cherbourg tomorrow? Be at the motor pool at 0800hrs, there is a convoy leaving for Cherbourg at 0830hrs, I have arranged room in a staff car."

"I'll be there," Henri assured.

"Thank you and goodnight," Heinrich said leaving the shop.

***

Henri arrived at the motor pool, which was very busy, with trucks and other vehicles coming from the damaged ship in the harbour.

"You there!" shouted a voice from a staff car. "You will be in this car."

It was not long before the convoy started moving, the journey was a long one. Henri tried to take in all he could see that might be of interest, occasionally falling asleep.

"Should be in time for dinner," said the driver waking Henri up with a start. "I'll drop you at the commandant's office".

The compound at Cherbourg was a hive of activity, vehicles of all types were being loaded, most of them had the desert colours and markings. *North Africa*, thought Henri, *I must try and find out when they leave and which route.*

"Mr Cartier, nice to meet you, I'm Commandant Krupp, I've heard a lot about your work. I'm hoping for a good portrait to put in pride of place in my home, my father has that position at the moment, so I want to make him proud."

Henri had a good meal, then went to bed and began writing what he could remember of the day's journey.

He woke early to a clear sky, the noise from the compound was gradually getting louder. He decided to start sketching straight away, just in case the vehicles moved.

"Excuse me, is it alright if I sit here, to get a feeling for the background to the commandant's painting?" Henri asked the young officer standing watching the loading of the trucks.

"We have orders to assist you all we can, just don't get in the way," the officer answered with a smirk.

The morning went very quickly, Henri sketched all he could of what was going on, watching the vehicles he became aware they were getting into some sort of convoy order.

The young officer walked over to him. "You will have to move now, we are closing this section for the rest of the day."

Henri packed his gear then asked, "will they be here tomorrow, as the commandant would like a busy background?"

"They will be here for two days, but the compound will be closed all day tomorrow, I suggest you finish here and get on with the commandant's portrait," remarked the young officer.

***

"Come," said the voice of the commandant, "how did the morning go?"

"Very well, nearly finished the rough background, could have done with a little more time but they have closed that part of the compound."

"Ah yes, busy time; we are loading all the trucks, so don't want you to get in the way. You can get started on me this afternoon."

Henri was getting on well and asked the commandant if any vehicle was going back to Fécamp the following morning, as it would be better to finish the portrait in his studio where he had all the paints he would need.

"A good idea, there is a car leaving at 0900hrs, I'll tell the driver; he only has one other passenger, a naval officer, he will be fine, like me an old school regular."

Henri thought that could be nice, at least a naval person, probably want speak but could be interesting. After a meal Henri worked on the painting before he fell asleep.

***

"Halt," the guard at the motor compound said as Henri approached.

"Going to Fécamp with a naval officer, told to report

here," Henri answered.

"Wait here you will be picked up shortly."

While waiting Henri took note of what was going on; he noticed ammunition boxes and water containers, stacked ready to be loaded.

"Vehicle coming," said the guard.

The car pulled up by the gate. "Any luggage?" the driver asked in a harsh voice.

"Only this here," Henri said pointing to his painting gear.

"In the boot," the driver demanded.

Henri got in the back, the naval officer looked at him. "The driver is a little sharp, apparently he is a relief driver, the one that should have been driving has to see a dentist, so this one is not too happy."

The journey went well, in between little periods of sleep Henri tried to find out what a naval captain would be going to Fécamp for.

Trying his luck Henri asked, "are you the captain of the damaged ship in the docks?"

"No, but I will be taking her elsewhere for repairs."

Henri did not push it any further.

They arrived at the compound in Fécamp late that evening.

"Take this gentleman home driver or he will be stopped, because of the curfew," the officer told him, "and thank you for a nice smooth ride."

Once at home Henri quickly started sketching what he could remember of Cherbourg and the compound, he worked through the night and managed to finish the rough copy of the vehicles and stores he saw at the compound, leaving out Commandant Krupp.

***

Henri woke with a jump, Pierre had arrived and was making coffee. "I wondered if you were back, I've bought some breakfast in case."

"Back late last night, finished a painting, must get it to the cove today."

"Did things go alright in Cherbourg?"

"Yes fine, I didn't go out of the compound."

"Take care out, there is a sergeant and two other soldiers getting drunk and picking on anybody, giving them a beating: men and women they don't care."

"I'll look out," answered Henri looking out the window at the damaged ship, wondering why they what it moved elsewhere.

Henri managed to get to the cove alright. He buried some dry clothes in the woods near to where he crossed the road to go down the pathway, he left the marker buoy in the usual place and returned to his shop.

"A good rest I think, then more painting," he said to Pierre as they sat enjoying a coffee.

CHAPTER 10

Chatham dockyard was getting busier, what with the air raids and constant movement of shipping, Roger Carter was certainly put in at the deep end.

"Another patrol tonight, suspect E-boat attack on our convoy coming down the coast from up north with much needed coal for factory's around the London area, we will pick it up near Boston and escort it into the Thames."

"How many ships sir?" asked Andrew Butcher, skipper of MTB884.

"Only six ships, but everyone is vital, the trains can't do it all, they are very busy so let's do our best. Right gentlemen see you all at 2130hrs for any updates."

Commander Wears left the Op's room while the skippers and their No1 got on with passage planning, they then checked the boat for ammunition and packed lunch, which was always welcome on a cold night.

It started to rain, the wind was coming from the north east. Cold and wet the six MTBs headed north up the coast, the spray was coming over the bridge, most of the crew were below waiting at any moment to be called to stations.

"I'll be glad to meet the convoy and turn about, enough to make you want shore duties," able seaman Lester said handing out some lunch packs.

Two hours passed before they met with the convoy. The escort vessels from Boston thanked them saying, "keep dry, no problems so far, safe journey home."

"I don't think we will have any distractions, the weather is getting worse," Roger said to the cox'n, "but I'll get the crew to stations now we have some slow charges."

Roger told the lookouts and the gun crews to be very alert. "Extra vigilant, it may be rough out there but I don't want any surprises."

It was nearly 0430hrs before the MTBs tied up onto their pontoons, the crews made for the showers and bed, Roger and his No1 made out the log before they also retired.

***

At Plymouth, Richard Carter was preparing his gun boat to do another pick up at the little cove.

"Everything ready Ginger?" Richard said to his No1.

"All taken care of skipper, and we have managed to remember to take the spare marker buoys, they may come in handy for your father."

This made Richard think about his father. "Yes they will help, I do worry about him."

"All set Carter," came a voice from the escort vessel, "leaving in five minutes."

Richard closed up the crew, "everyone be extra alert tonight, it looks like we may have quite a spell of moonlight."

Leaving the escort vessel, the gun boat headed towards the French coast, once passed the halfway Richard ordered slow ahead; usual practice as at night a bow wave can be seen from a distance.

Time passed slowly, everyone was looking into the darkness. "Silhouette on port bow skipper," reported the bridge gunner.

Richard and all the lookouts trained their eyes on the shape. "Looks like a warship. Stop engines, let it pass; total silence."

Half an hour passed before Richard gave the order slow ahead.

"Let's hope there are no more about," said the cox'n.

Gradually the gun boat moved closer to the French coast.

"Coast line port bow, Seaman Darby get ready," Richard said to Darby who had just came onto the bridge.

"Ready skipper, the tides should be better as we are early."

Seaman Darby was lowered over the side. "Take these marker buoys and leave them at the pickup point."

Once Darby was clear of the boat Richard told the cox'n to turn about and get out to sea.

Darby could see the big rock ahead, the sea was quite choppy which made the going hard. Reaching the rock Darby rested for a few moments before looking for the buoy, he suddenly froze, a light was searching along and around the little cove.

Richard had also seen the light. "Stand by guns," he whispered, "just in case."

Seaman Darby noticed two soldiers looking among the rocks, and getting closer. He kept very still hoping the big rock hid him.

Time passed which seemed endless before the light moved up to the road and stopped, a sound of a car moving away made Darby feel better. He found the marker buoy, retrieved it and left the others. He checked all was clear and headed back to the gunboat.

The way back was a little scary as the moonlight shone on a wide area of sea.

Richard moved the boat closer inshore, aware of the moonlight. "Canoe ahead, get ready to bring Darby aboard, and get the canoe stowed quickly."

"That was close, looks like they were looking for something," Richard remarked as seaman Darby was hauled aboard. "Slow ahead cox'n, let's go home. Well done Darby."

Once out at sea the MGB put the power on and was soon heading towards home.

***

Henri Cartier finished the painting of Commandant Krupp, he turned to Pierre saying how much information was in the background. "I've never really noticed it before, but looking at it there's a lot of detail, I'm very pleased. Tomorrow I will take it to Cherbourg, so look after everything, I want to see this one finished."

Next morning Henri was walking to the compound when a German officer called his name, turning around it was the officer he had met before: firstly at the cove, and also at the compound.

"I'm going to the compound to see if I can get a lift to Cherbourg, I've finished the painting of Commandant Krupp."

"I'll walk with you, I'm going there. The painting of Commander Fullier was very good, he can't stop showing everyone."

"I'm glad he liked it," Henri said as they reached the gates.

"Tell me Henri has anyone been complaining about being assaulted by a sergeant and two other soldiers?"

"We have leant not to complain because of reprisals," Henri answered, wondering why he was asked.

"That is not what all of us believe, if I tell you what I've heard, you tell me if it's true; a sergeant and two others from the motor pool get drunk most nights, refusing to pay for their drinks then on the way back to the motor pool would pick on anyone they saw: true or false?"

"True, it's very difficult, people are the same all over and it's only time before harm comes to them," Henri answered as they entered the compound.

"I understand, please have faith in me, I will see it never happens again."

Commander Fullier said a convoy was leaving around 1800hrs and asked Henri if he could be back at 1745hrs.

"Thank you I'll be here," Henri replied.

After a long tiring journey Henri arrived at the compound in Cherbourg, he went straight to the admin office asking to see Commandant Krupp.

"Good day Cartier, come in," said a voice from inside the office marked *Commandant*.

"I have your painting, I think you will like it," Henri said placing the painting on the desk by the window which overlooked a good section of the dockyard.

Commandant Krupp had a good look at the painting.

"Now that I like very much, you work quickly for so much detail."

"I did work two days and most of the nights, I wanted to get it finished as I have other work," replied Henri.

"It will look grand at home, most impressive."

"Thank you Commandant, I would like to go into town to an art shop I know to get some more paints."

"Allow me to buy them, as well as something for the painting," Commandant Krupp offered.

***

Henri was glad to get out of the compound, he walked to the art shop he knew taking in all he saw. Buying what he needed he headed back, unaware his ex-wife and her partner Philippe Du'rio had been outside a shoe shop opposite.

Surprised to see him, Yvette Du'rio, as she was now known, followed. Henri walked through the compound gate and directly to the admin office.

Yvette watched, this confused her and Philippe. "What do you think he is doing?" she asked.

"I don't know but tomorrow I will find out. Tonight we are dining with some important people, we have to go and change."

***

Henri got his lift back to Fécamp that evening.

"All go well?" Pierre asked.

"Yes I think so, there was some interesting shipping movements and a lot of army vehicles painted for North Africa, I'd better get all this down while it's fresh and get to the cove."

"I'll get some dinner so you can get on," Pierre remarked.

Henri worked most of that night, and the next day, he finally finished at 1730hrs, packing what he wanted in the buoy. He waited another hour until it was dark, then made his way to the cove and checked all was clear before moving down the path. Once out of site from the road he waded towards the big rock, exchanged the buoys, then made for some rocks which were well hidden from the road.

Henri put his dry clothes on, and decided to wait and see if a pick up would come that night.

***

"Prepare the canoe," Richard said quietly. "Get ready Darby, nearly there; usual drill."

The gunboat moved closer to shore before Darby set off, he reached the big rock and soon found the buoy.

All this was watched by Henri until the canoe was out of site. *Was that the slightest sound of a gunboat, or just the wind playing tricks?*

Henri managed to get back to the shop without being seen and had a hot drink before going to bed.

CHAPTER 11

Henri woke with a jump; to the sound of his front door being knocked open.

Two German soldiers with automatic guns burst into his bedroom. "Get dressed now!" one shouted.

Down stairs he was confronted by the German officer he knew as Heinrich Mass.

"What's this all about?" he asked.

"Henri Cartier, or should I call you Henry Carter? You have been reported as being a British spy, doing what I don't know. Can you give me an explanation? I have orders to hand you over to the SS."

"And who may I ask put forward this information?"

"I'm *sure* you want like the answer. It's not any of the locals; while you were in Cherbourg you were seen by a Mrs Yvette Du'rio, your ex-wife, now working for the

German propaganda ministry with her husband Philippe Du'rio."

Henri looked at the German officer, "can't much argue with that."

Henri was put in the back of the car with Heinrich.

"Nothing I could have done," he said quietly. "A wife's betrayal is hard to take."

Arriving at the compound Henri was handed straight over to the SS.

Heinrick Mass went back to the shop, where Pierre had just arrived. "What's happened?" he asked.

"Henri has been arrested for spying, the SS has him. Now I would suggest you go home as the SS will do a search of the shop, then I will lock it up and make it secure."

Pierre went home wondering how Henri was and what will happen to him. *I must try and let the British know* he thought as he made his way to where Ramond Le'tore, the police sergeant, was always having a coffee.

The police sergeant told Pierre that if the SS had Henri and they thought the claims to be true then he would be shot as a spy. "How did they find out?"

"I don't know, that young German officer came and told me, and said to keep away for now as the SS are involved."

Ramond said he would make some enquiries. "That young officer often speaks, he was a trainee teacher and not into military affairs, he's what I call an organiser."

"How can I let the British know? Henri didn't tell me what he was doing at the cove, something to with marker buoys, but I don't know which department he works for."

"Leave it to me, I'll get a message to England," Ramond said as they both walked back, past the shop.

CHAPTER 12

Nine days passed, and after two trips to the cove and nothing to pick up, Commander Knight called Richard to his office.

"Richard, I think tonight instead of your diver I want you to go ashore and see if you can find out what's going on, very unusual nothing for so long."

"Very good sir, Ginger Gibbons can bring the boat back."

"That's fine, Gibbons will pick you up two nights from now at the same place, if you are not there he will try two nights later. Be careful in case something has gone wrong, and remember if you are not there on the second pick up, you will have to contact us somehow and we will try once more," Commander Knight said shaking Richard's hand and wishing him good luck.

***

"Escort vessel ready skipper," said Ginger Gibbons. "Now have you got all you should have: clothing money, washing gear papers etc.?"

"Yes all set, let's go," Richard said taking his position on the bridge.

"Escort vessel signalled, bon voyage," said the bridge lookout.

"Thank you Thomas," Richard answered.

"Cox'n usual heading, you have the con Ginger, call me when near, I'm checking everything."

The crossing was pretty rough, which probably was better for the gunboat as they never saw any other vessel.

"Coast in sight skipper," Ginger told Richard. "Hope the new fold up canoe is stable enough in this sea."

"Thank you Ginger, the boat's all yours, look after her. See you the night after next."

After a short hand shake and a look back at his boat Richard disappeared into the darkness.

Ginger Gibbons stood on the bridge looking into the night, turned to the cox'n. "Let's go home slowly for now until well clear, lookouts anything to report?"

"Nothing sir, all clear," said a lookout, as the gunboat headed out to sea.

***

Richard came alongside the big rock, looked for the best place to come ashore, finding a gap between some rocks he managed to get the canoe well hidden in a small overhanging cave. *That should do* he thought as he gathered his gear and made for the path he knew well. He knew there was probably a curfew in place, and he must be careful: don't rush, take plenty of time to check all is clear, and he must keep to the wooded part as much as he could.

Richard was just entering the promenade section of the town when an army vehicle came around a corner not far from him, he quickly jumped among some rubbish that had been left out ready for collection. The vehicle drove passed, Richard slowly made sure all was clear then made his way to the shop.

Reaching the shop he was surprised to find it secured with a chain and padlock, he thought for a while then remembered the back entrance, which was in a narrow passage way. Going through a small gate he looked at the back door, probably well locked from the inside.

Richard remembered a toilet window above the outhouse, climbing onto the roof of the outhouse he took out his pistol and smashed the small window. "Just about enough room to get in," he said to himself. Clearing the glass away he managed to get inside, he switched on his torch and made for the bedroom, which had been ransacked. He made himself a hot drink, made up a bed and fell asleep.

Waking early Richard had a good look around the shop, everything had been turned upside down. *I must go and see if Pierre is still around* he thought. Seeing a marker buoy under a workbench Richard looked at it, inside was a tube with a painting in it; he noticed a note attached to the painting - *one that never got delivered to the cove.*

***

Henri Cartier was arrested, and taken to the SS. He was shot as a British agent. He was betrayed by his ex-wife Yvette Du'rio,

who saw him in Cherbourg. I will try and get this message to
England. Pierre.

Richard sat with tears in his eyes, how could his mother have done this? He made a strong coffee, put the note in his pocket and went to see Pierre.

"Richard come in quickly," Pierre said, surprised to see him.

"I saw the note," Richard said, showing Pierre. "What happened?"

"It all happened so quickly, some Germans came early in the morning and took him to the SS HQ. The next day he was shot by firing squad, a young German officer came and told me. He said Henri was seen in Cherbourg by your mother and she went to the authorities; she is working for the German propaganda department. I was going to take the note and the painting to the little cove, but wasn't sure what to do with it." Pierre said. "If I knew what the marker buoys were used for I could continue doing the same without the German portrait in it."

"Pierre when this is all over, the shop is all yours; I'm sure Father would have liked that."

While Pierre was getting some breakfast Richard told

him about the pickup, and where to place the marker buoys. "Do you know where my mother might be now?" he asked Pierre.

"I'll try and find out, you be very careful and keep out of sight in case your mother is still around."

"I have to be at the cove tomorrow, I'll take the note and painting. I'll stay in the shop tonight and sort out anything of Father's before I have to go back to England."

***

Turning the corner by the shop, Richard stopped; outside the shop was a police bicycle and a policeman opening the padlock.

Richard crossed the road to the next corner, stood in a doorway and watched. He noticed that the policeman was his father's friend, Ramond Le'tore.

Dare I speak? he thought. *I must to see what's going on.*

"Sergeant Le'tore, can I help you?" Richard said keeping one hand in his pocket by his revolver.

The sergeant turned with a startled look. "I thought you were your father, you sound alike." The padlock came off and Ramond opened the door. "Quickly inside, the Germans will be here shortly, what are you doing here?" he asked.

"To find out what happened to my father. Now I know I'm going to find my mother and face her."

"Richard shortly a car will arrive from German HQ, in it will be your mother and her husband, they are sorting your father's things for any clues to what he was up to. I would suggest you go out the back way and go to Pierre's house, out the way for now, I'm locking the shop again at 1800hrs, look after yourself."

Richard left through the back, propping the door with a length of timber he found in the yard. He pulled his woollen hat well down over his head and went round the block to the other side of the road by some empty crates so he could watch the shop. He decided it was too exposed, and went back to Pierre's house.

Richard told Pierre what had happened, and how he had spoken to Ramond Le'tore. "I'm going back to the shop shortly, and what I do after that depends on what happens when I get there. Whatever does happen you should keep away, have a word with Le'tore. Pierre take care of yourself, hope to see you after all this."

Shaking Pierre's hand Richard left, heading for the shop. He saw that there was no car so waited once again by the crates. An hour passed before a German staff car pulled up outside the shop, out stepped a German officer and Philippe Du'rio, then the back door opened and out stepped his mother, she was laughing as they entered the shop.

Richard waited wondering what to do next when the German officer came out of the shop and drove away. Moving closer to the shop he saw his mother standing by the counter looking at some paperwork. He went around to the back, carefully removed the timber bearer and quietly entered the back room.

"Whatever he was up to must be here somewhere," Philippe was saying to Yvette.

"He must have been spying, no other reason for him to have been here. Keep looking," Yvette said.

A sound behind made them both jump.

As she turned around Yvette's face dropped. "Richard what are you doing here?" she said in a shaky voice.

Richard stood holding his revolver pointed at Philippe.

"I've heard a lot about you since you ran off with this traitor to France, and you a traitor to England," he told his mother in a calm voice, but inwardly shaking.

"Richard you don't understand, we have a good position with the Germans, who will win the war, look how easy it has been so far. England will be next. You can be a part of it. Put down the gun and help us," said Yvette, holding out her arms.

"I do understand Mother, sorry." With that Richard fired two shots, then went out the back way, locking the door as he left. He headed for the little cove and knew he had a long wait until tomorrow night before the pickup.

***

Two hours passed before Heinrick Mass returned to the shop, where he found was the bodies of Yvette and Philippe on the floor; Yvette had a note covering her face.

This is my revenge on my mother and her husband Philippe Du'rio for betraying my father, her ex-husband. God save the King. Signed Lt. Richard Carter RN.

Heinrich told his driver to go to the compound and get a

truck to remove the bodies.

When Sergeant Le'tore entered the shop, he looked at the scene said nothing to Heinrich, who showed him the note. Within an hour the town was full of soldiers and check points were put up everywhere.

***

Richard had made it to the cove and hid himself among the rocks, he was glad he had brought a heavy coat and a blanket and knew he had a long wait.

All that day he heard sounds coming from the town, he just hoped nobody was getting hurt.

It was about 0200hrs the next morning when Richard retrieved the canoe and started paddling out toward the pickup, soon he heard the purr of the gun boat.

"Canoe sighted sir," a lookout said quietly.

"Good pick him up and get the canoe stowed, then let's get out of here," Ginger told the crew standing by the guns.

Once on board Richard told Ginger to rev her up. "I want them to know we were here."

All this was witnessed by the young German officer. *I would have done the same* Heinrich Mass thought putting away his binoculars. He got back into his car he headed back to Fécamp.

CHAPTER 13

Heinrich Mass entered the commandant's office early next morning.

"Everything is tidied up, the old man Pierre, he has worked at the shop since he was a young man, the previous owners sold the shop to Henri Cartier with the understanding Pierre was kept on, I can see no problem with him carrying on with the shop, less for us to worry about. We have searched the premises and nothing incriminating was found, only a couple of unfinished paintings which Pierre said he would complete, I would say episode closed."

The commandant thought for a while. "I think so too, tell this Pierre he can continue trading, any news on this Lt. Richard Carter?"

"No news, I should imagine well gone," Heinrich

replied.

"Fine Heinrich, episode closed."

***

Back at Plymouth Richard was called to HQ office to see Admiral Webster.

"Lt. Carter to see you sir," said the marine at the door.

"Come in Lt. I believe you know Commander Knight."

Richard shook hands, wondering what was going on.

Admiral Webster said he was sorry about his father, and asked if he had been able to find out what had happened.

Richard explained and told them what he had done. There was a little silence then Commander Knight said, "A sad thing to do, but I'm sure we would have done the same. You have a strong character, and that is why we would like you to get involved with the French underground at Brest, as you know it's a submarine base and full of Germans, not an easy place to operate from. If you are willing to except we will give your No1 Lt Ginger Gibbons your boat, I think he is capable."

"Ginger's fine I'd recommend him, so tell me more about

this job?" Richard asked.

"Submarines are housed in pens of thick concrete and well guarded, your job is to let us know of comings and goings of submarines and troop movements around that area."

"How will I let you know?" Richard remarked thinking about the place crawling with Germans.

"There is a resistance movement operating around Brest, we are informed they are real loyal Frenchmen, they have a radio, but it's very limited, we have a new type maybe experimental at the moment but very good. It has a very high frequency, plus it's quite small and can easily be carried around, to listen on a normal receiver all you would hear is a hum, but with the receiver we have it operates well, ideal for that area as a lot of radio traffic goes in and out of there."

"Will the locals be expecting me?" Richard asked.

"Yes, a man named Lauri Fern will meet you at the drop point, you will live with him and his daughter Marie. They will help you with whatever you do, good people, he was educated in England; an engineer I believe," remarked the admiral.

"When do I leave? At least I know Brest very well," said Richard.

"Another reason you are suited for the job. I suggest you brush up on the new machine as it is very delicate. You leave, weather permitting, the night after next; you will be taken by plane to a small town called St. Brieuc, we are doing an air raid on the coastal town of St. Nazaire, the aircraft will make a slight detour to drop you. Tomorrow you will have one practice jump, some safety, and survival training. Any questions?"

***

Richard woke with a start. "Morning sir, breakfast in fifteen minutes, then some safety lessons. Vehicle will pick you up at 0900hrs," said the burly RAF sergeant.

"Thank you I'll be ready."

The morning went well, a few embarrassing moments but Richard was pleased; he hit the target eight out of ten shots with his pistol but with the sten gun he missed most of the target.

"If you have to use it you will probably do better, it will

come. Lunch break then we go and get ready for your one and only jump before the real thing. Oh, and just one thing; the real jump will be in darkness." A little smirk appeared on the sergeant's face.

***

"Ready sir?" said the navigator. "Just coming up to the drop zone, remember your chute will open automatically. Feet together, arms crossed, GO!"

Richard was enjoying the floating feeling, until he realised he could not see the ground. Suddenly two lights came into view just on his right hand side, turning the straps to the right he pulled down hard, a little too late; he hit the ground quite hard, rolling over before coming to a halt.

Richard saw three people coming towards him as he struggled to get out of the parachute harness.

"Richard Carter?" said a voice as they came closer.

"Yes," said Richard as another man and a woman helped pack the parachute in a bag.

"Glad you made it alright, we had better get clear of here

in case anyone saw or heard you. I'm Lauri Fern, this is my daughter Marie and this is Antoine, a friend."

They soon arrived at a small house on the edge of St. Brieuc. It was old with crumbling walls, but once inside Richard felt the cosy home atmosphere of a house that was lived in.

Richard thanked Lauri for allowing him to stay.

"We have a nice little room for you," said Marie, "its behind the pantry wall."

Richard was shown how the pantry door opened, on one side was pots and pans, and some tin food, the other side was cleaning materials. At the back, which looked just like a wall, Marie pushed and it opened into a small but tidy little room, with bed, wash basin, and a bucket with lid. "Just for you," Marie said as she showed Richard the chest of drawers.

"This will do nicely," Richard remarked, putting his bag on the bed.

"Now a hot drink and something to eat, then a few hours rest," replied Lauri.

***

Richard woke to the sound of voices coming from the kitchen.

"Good morning, did you sleep alright?" Marie asked.

"Yes thank you, what's on the agenda for today?"

"First some breakfast," Lauri said coming into the kitchen. "I have just had a friend call, he told me the Germans have a large convoy of torpedoes and ammunition coming this way, going to Brest."

"Do you sabotage anything like that?" Richard asked.

"No, usually a big convoy is too well escorted, but I think it would be a good idea if we could notify the British, they might like to do a bombing run on it. As soon as we know where it's coming from and which route we can send a message," Lauri answered.

Two hours later, Lauri's friend Claude returned. "The convoy is going to Brest, it's armament for the submarines. At present the route is Lyon to Tours and then to Rennes, once passed Tours we will know which route it will take to Brest, Rennes is the probable one as it's much flatter and with better roads."

"As soon as it's passed Tours you can send the message,

the RAF would still have plenty of time to catch the convoy at Rennes," Lauri said to Richard.

"If I send a message now to pre-warn them they could be ready," explained Richard.

Marie told Richard to bring his new transmitter and they headed into the woods, quite away from the house. As soon as they arrived at a small clearing Marie stopped, saying, "this is an ideal spot: it's high ground and not too much interference. You don't get many German soldiers here, word was spread around that poachers shoot Germans as well."

Richard set up his transmitter, tuned it to the very high frequency required and wrote a message on a pad. "Right Marie," he said, "let's see if I can get this message off."

Richard tapped out the message. *Ammunition convoy on route from Lyon to Brest, via Tours, Rennes, to Brest. With torpedoes, and ammunition. Will confirm route from Tours ASAP. RC.*

"I didn't hear any of that, just a high pitched tone," said Marie.

"That's the idea, now let's get back to the house," Richard answered, packing up the transmitter.

CHAPTER 14

"Signal from RC," said the operator, "it's come through on the new type of machine."

The duty petty officer took the message to Admiral Webster's office. "Signal from RC sir."

"So the machine works," he said as he read the message. Reading it again he called his secretary. "Assemble the team to the wardroom in ten minutes."

***

Admiral Webster entered the wardroom and spread out a map of France on the table.

"Gentlemen you will be pleased to know our new radio seems to work alright, I have just received a signal from our man in France; a large convoy of ammunition and torpedoes are heading for Brest, and we all know what's at Brest."

"If the convoy delivers, not good news for our shipping," replied a commander.

"Quite," Admiral Webster answered. "We must have a go at stopping it," he said, turning to his secretary. "Call the RAF chap, Wing Commander Blake, and ask him to come over right away."

An hour later Wing Commander Blake was brought up to date so far, and told the admiral that as soon as he received the exact route and times at each check point he could work out where the convoy should be in about eight hours time.

"I will have six Blenheim bombers ready in two hours, so that should give them time. Right gentlemen I await your call."

The Wing Commander left to arrange his plans.

"Blenheim bombers are well equipped for jobs like this, and they have a good turn of speed, I think they are the best option," remarked the Admiral.

Just over an hour later the wing commander rang. "Hello Admiral, planes are ready and standing by waiting for the off, the crews are resting, the weather looks kind, so we now just wait."

"As soon as I hear I'll let you know, and thank you."

***

Richard made his way to the woods with Marie, keeping well to the thick wooded parts. They soon arrived at the place Marie had chosen. "Keep a good lookout while I send," Richard told Marie getting the transmitter ready.

Signal from RC sir. Confirm previous route, ETA tours 0315hrs. Follow railway line towards Rennes, convoy ETA Rennes 0600hrs. RC out.

***

The six Blenheim bombers crossed the English Channel at low altitude, which the Blenheim bombers were famous for; the morning mist was welcome.

"Coast coming up keep sharp lads, look out for any aircraft or ground fire," said Sqd. Leader Fallows.

Flt. Lt. Gary Smith, Fallow's wing man, radioed. "I can

see the main road just south of the railway line leader."

Following the railway line for another twelve minutes, Fallows passed the word, "convoy sighted straight ahead."

The early morning light was just rising, ideal for a dawn attack. Sqd. Leader Fallows radioed, "on my mark, single file follow me."

The six bombers roared along the road, one after the other, firing all guns and dropping their bombs among the trucks. Their cannon fire ripped the convoy apart, trucks exploded, ammunition trucks burst into flames, it was all over in eight minutes.

"Well done chaps, all planes head home, fly high, I expect some company going back."

All six Blenheims returned safety. Sqd. Leader Fallows reported damage looked severe, but only people on the ground could give the exact amount.

Word came through to Lauri Fern that only three trucks were not destroyed, and they had ammunition, and supplies, all the torpedo trucks were blown up, a good job well done.

"Good, that's less to worry about," Richard remarked.

"Wonder if the Germans will make any sort of reprisal?

We had better keep low for a little while until we know," Lauri answered

"I'll let those in England know how the raid went," Richard said getting ready to go to the woods.

Marie soon found the spot where Richard had hidden the transmitter, Richard was setting it up when Marie suddenly put her hand over Richard's mouth.

"Germans coming this way, they are probably looking for the man from the next village who killed a German soldier for hitting his 8 year old son."

They found a good hiding place and waited until the patrol was well passed before sending the message.

Back in Plymouth Admiral Webster called his team, and read the signal. "Convoy 90% destroyed, only two ammunition trucks and one supply truck undamaged, well done. RC out."

Admiral Webster thanked the wing commander for the success. "Those Blenheim bombers do a marvellous job thank you again, a few less torpedoes for our ships to worry about."

***

Two days passed with nothing from the German HQ in Brest.

"They probably thought it was spotted leaving Lyon," Lauri said over breakfast.

"I think I should have a look around Brest today, I know the place well, but not the people or where to stay," Richard replied, thinking of the submarine pens.

Lauri thought for a while. "We have a cousin there, not far from the docks, Marie will go with you to introduce you, it's not an easy place to get into."

Marie said to Richard the best way was by train. "It leaves about 1400hrs if it's on time, don't take much gear, the Germans look for anyone with lots, the best is for us to take vegetables, and say it is for our relations. Your radio you will have to hide somehow, I'll give you a walking stick, so you can walk with a limp."

Lauri wished them well and good luck, regards to Alf.

The train left forty minutes late, with quite a lot of people, mainly farmers with their products, w Marie and Richard were able to mix in.

About half an hour went by when a railway official and

two German guards came into the carriage. "Papers."

Richard put his radio under his seat, covering it with his coat.

The guard stopped at a young man sitting near a door. "What is this?" he said.

The two guards approached, the young man jumped up drew a revolver and pushed the two Germans over, a crowd of people made it hard for them to get up quickly while the young man escaped out of the carriage door and ran towards the woods.

Four German soldiers from the carriage behind and the two from Marie's jumped off the train and ran after the man.

Richard watched as the young man disappeared into the woods. The guard came up to Marie. "I think if you and your friend go into the carriage behind, I've checked that one."

"What was that all about?" Richard asked.

"That young man and a few others do that sort of thing, to distract the Germans from searching for something they might find. In this case it was your friend here, I was pre warned and young Le'vac said he would do it."

"Thank you uncle Leo," Marie said giving him a peck on the cheek.

The train arrived at Brest with no further incidents, they had no trouble getting out of the station and went straight to Marie's cousin's house.

"Hello uncle Alf," said Marie.

"Marie, come in and who is this? Your young man? How is your father? What brings you to Brest, or maybe I should not ask?"

Marie explained why they were there, and asked if they could they stay a few days.

"Of course you can stay, but be very careful in Brest, it's full of soldiers and sailors."

Over supper, Marie told her uncle what had happened on the train, and about the raid on the convoy.

"I heard about the convoy, the RAF done a good job so I hear, I expect the submarine boys were counting on those torpedoes and ammunition," Alf said pouring another glass of local wine. "Helps you sleep."

Marie told her uncle all what was going on in Morgat and St. Brieuc.

"I've made the bed up in the spare room, it's a cosy room

and you can see the whole street from the window."

Marie looked at Richard. "I think he believes we are a couple, I know he only has two bedrooms, I expect we can manage."

Richard told Marie she would have the bed and he would be fine on the floor. "Just like a ship's bunk," he joked. "I'll be up most of the night, I have some notes to do."

"There's plenty of room in the bed, don't argue, when you have finished, just get in and get some sleep," Marie answered with a smile.

It was after midnight before Richard stopped writing, he walked to the window, looking at Marie who was fast asleep, he looked up and down the street; in the distance he could hear activity at the docks.

He looked up and down once again; nothing about. He put his coat on and slipped quietly out of the house, heading towards the dock area keeping well to the shadows. The sound of a service vehicle passing on their way to the docks made him sink into a dark corner.

Turning a corner the dock gates came into view, guards everywhere.

Richard made his way to a point he knew which overlooked the docks and part of the submarine pens. Writing down all he could see loaded and unloaded from trucks and small coasters, he noticed a trolley with some torpedoes being pulled by a small truck which disappeared into a concrete building.

Time to go he said to himself, heading back once again keeping to the shadows. Marie was still asleep, Richard eased himself into the bed and soon fell asleep.

CHAPTER 15

The days went by. Richard and Marie had been busy gathering all they could on what was happening in Brest.

"I have to try and find out how thick the concrete pens are, and if a bomb could damage them," Richard said to Alf.

"I think the pens are bomb proof, some of the locals worked on the construction," Alf answered.

Talking it over with Alf, Richard decided to radio Plymouth with the information so far; that he believed the pens to be bomb proof.

"Signal from RC sir."

Admiral Webster read it. "Reply that I am sending expert bomb disposal sergeant from the engineer's special forces, he is used to operating behind enemy lines, he will look and check it out. Suggest drop zone square 6 of your map, at 0010hrs tomorrow morning."

Richard and Marie left early for the drop zone, as it was quite a large area and they wanted to get into a position with which to have the best view, and to make sure nobody was around.

"Aircraft noise," Marie whispered.

"I hear, it sounds like a Lysander light aircraft, look out for a parachute," Richard answered.

"There," pointed Marie, just over that hedge.

They both ran the 200 yards or more to where the chute had landed, suddenly a figure appeared from behind a mound holding a sten gun.

"I'm Richard Carter, this is Marie Fern."

"I'm Sergeant Derek Myers."

Richard and Derek rolled up the parachute and put it in a bag. "We will bury it in the woods, we have all today to get sorted and tell you what we know and all about the local layout. Tomorrow morning at 0730hrs we catch the train for Brest," explained Richard.

"Straight into it, no wasting time," Derek answered.

"We have to, once the Germans think a resistance group is operating in the area they tighten everything which make it hard to get about," Marie replied.

The following morning came quickly, Marie had told Derek how the train journey was the best way to get to Brest as the roads often had road blocks.

"The train is usually full with market traders, we should blend in."

Richard explained that they would eat bread and cheese on the train like everyone else. "Keeps the mouth full in case any German asks for any papers, then someone will answer in French, by the time you clear your mouth the Germans go, they have a whole train to walk through and don't like hanging about."

The journey was very quiet. Derek told Richard what he would be looking for: what type of concrete, how many layers of wire, how thick, angle of layers etc. "It all adds up to what sort of explosive should be used, you can usually tell what something is made of by the spare material lying around."

The guards around the dock area seemed unusually heavy. "I wonder what's going on," said Richard.

"Maybe a VIP visit," Marie muttered.

"That could be interesting, let's walk around the block

and see if we can get a better view," Derek was saying when they suddenly came to a halt. A barrier had been put across the road, with soldiers everywhere. They were just wondering which way to go, when a convoy went past with a big staff car in the middle. Richard could just make out the uniform of an Admiral sitting in the back. "That's an Admiral he must be visiting the pens."

When all was clear the barriers were removed, and the road open again. They spent the next hour looking at the pens from different directions, noting what material was lying around, Derek was making plenty of notes. "I think I've seen enough, I don't think bombing will do enough damage, let's go."

***

Back at Alf's house Derek, Richard and Marie sat down to discuss what they could make of the pens.

"I don't think I could get anywhere near to plant any explosives that would have any impact: tight security, no chance of a land operation. I'll make my report and leave it the powers to be."

"Maybe we could hijack a German sub, wait for another to go in, follow it and once inside fire all torpedoes," said Richard, making them all laugh.

"I'll send my report tonight," Derek said as Alf bought them all in a bowl of thick vegetable soup.

CHAPTER 16

The powers in Plymouth decided that a sustained attack once again by Blenheim bombers should be enough to cripple the pens for a while.

Sqd. Leader Fallows was asked how many bombers could be ready by tomorrow night, as the weather looked right: low cloud which suited the Blenheims as they fly low over their targets then disappear into the cloud cover.

"I can have eight ready right now, all we have to do is load the bombs and re-arm," the station commander told the Admiral.

"Good then, tomorrow night, I'll let our boys on the ground know what's happening."

***

"We must keep well clear of the dock area tomorrow night, there's an air raid taking place and they want us to send a report back on how it went," said Richard.

Derek said he would word it in his unit's terms, scale 1 to 10 on each pen and surrounding buildings.

"Good idea Derek, now I believe Alf has some news for us, let's eat."

Alf entered with two other men, who he introduced as loyal Frenchmen, one spread a map on the table.

"This is the railway line from Bordeaux to Brest, it goes via Nantes, we have information a train will leave Bordeaux tomorrow night carrying torpedoes and ammunition; it should pass through Nantes about 0300hrs. What we would like is your sergeant to come with us and help to derail it at Redon, there is a large factory there making bombs, if the train went off at the bend that bypasses the factory it should roll down the embankment into the store room. We would like to have the train blown up if possible".

A silence, before Derek asked if they had enough explosives and fuse wire, and how would he get to Redon.

"We have all the gear you will need, but we lack the

knowledge on how to use it, we would hope you could show us?" the other man said. "We would have to leave now."

***

The following morning Richard and Marie were walking near the dock area, barriers were being put up all around the approach roads.

"A lot of activity about today," said Marie.

"Yes, let's get home and see if Alf has found anything."

Alf was talking to two friends when Richard arrived. "Richard, they are closing all the roads and putting on extra guards. This afternoon a high ranking official including some head of security for this area are here to welcome a new long range submarine, it's due about 1700hrs. Inside information has said it may have to wait outside by the sea wall until there's a spare bay, at present the pens are full, busy loading."

"That's interesting, might make tonight's raid even more important, I'll radio Plymouth," Richard replied.

***

Sqd. Leader Fallows gave the final briefing to the eight crews. "Red section to drop their bombs from harbour entrance to pens opening, hopefully one might find its way inside, all the time firing your cannons. Blue section do the same, remainder straddle the buildings on each side. I will lead the port side buildings, we believe somewhere in one of the buildings is a control centre. Once you have released your bombs climb high and head for home, and good luck gentlemen."

Sqd. Leader Fallows and his eight Blenheim bombers were soon crossing the channel at low altitude.

Richard meanwhile had ventured out to see what was happening, the officials had moved into the main building, celebrating the arrival of the long range submarine and its crew. Guards were everywhere. He decided to head for a vantage point about a mile away on the edge of a breakwater; a good view of the pens, and well hidden from anyone passing.

After an hour and ten minutes he wished he had brought a big coat, a chill wind with dark skies made the waiting for the raid even more eerie. Suddenly the peace came to an end: sirens began their wailing, then came the sound of aircraft firing their cannons and the sound of bombs. The sky was a bright orange colour, big flashes of high explosives, then came the sound of the German guns.

Richard covered his ears while watching the carnage. Sqd. Leader Fallows took out the buildings alongside the pens, red section and blue section made a mess of the entrance to the pens, damaging the new doors and destroying the new long range submarine. The rest of the buildings were destroyed, the pens themselves were only slightly damaged.

It was all over in minutes the aircraft disappeared into the night, the guns had stopped, the whole area was a blazing mess.

Richard headed back to the house to find windows broken but no real damage.

Sergeant Myers left for Nantes with the two Frenchmen early morning. "Hope to see you when I get back."

They all wished him well and told him to take care.

Richard said he would get a report off to Plymouth. "I think it has put them back a little, admin block and other buildings destroyed, pens will soon be fixed."

Next morning the whole dock area was full of troops clearing the damaged buildings and keeping the roads clear.

Alf said he would try and find out what damage there was from his friend Francoise, who looked after one of the gates.

It was nearly 3 p.m. before Alf returned with Francoise.

"The new submarine was totally destroyed; it is now in bits on the bottom by pen No4, so no subs in our out until they have cleared it. The VIPs that were celebrating had gone to their accommodation for the night, a lot of ambulances were about and I hear one VIP is in hospital, two are definitely dead, my friend at the hospital is going to find out who it is."

"Well that's not bad. Let's make a note and I'll send that to Plymouth, we must get everything down ready to send, then I suggest we keep out of the way for awhile," Richard said.

The rest of the day was spent eating, drinking and talking about old times.

CHAPTER 17

Sergeant Derek Myers and the two Frenchmen, Bart and Renee, arrived near Nantes early in the evening, having spent the early morning and that day travelling from Brest. Their old work truck was full of wood and tools.

They had been stopped many times. "What have you there?" they were always asked.

"We mend barns and out buildings, and sell fire wood," Renee would say, that worked, but often the truck was searched, which took time.

"We have a place to stay," Bart said turning the old truck into a local council yard. "There is a big office and some smaller rooms, we can have the two rooms at the back, they have a back exit, just in case we need it."

They settled into a room which had a large table and six chairs. Bart spread his map on the table, Renee had a big piece of paper and pencil. "We are expecting some more locals who would like you to show them what to do, they are loyal and willing to learn."

Soon the small room looked crowded, there were nine other Frenchmen all gathered around the table. Bart with his paper and pencil began drawing the train track, and where the train slowed down to turn the sharp bend alongside the factory. "This looks like the best place to derail the train, in the buildings next to the slopping bank is where they store bombs, ammunition and warheads for the torpedoes."

"Will there be any civilians in the buildings?" Derek asked.

"Not at that time of night, there will be only guards," said one man. "My uncle operates the overhead crane and told me everyone finishes at 8 p.m."

"What about reprisals?" Derek asked.

"We cope with that, the Germans have always thought trouble comes from the big cities."

Derek explained what he would need if they wish to go ahead. "What I would suggest is, just as the train engine passes the bend and straightens that is the best place to derail it as the weight of the rest will carry it over the embankment, and all the carriages should follow. Now how to go about it, can someone manage to undo a joint of railway track?"

A long silence. "Yes my brother and I can do that," said another man.

"Good, you will need to undo both sides of the track and Jemmy them to the right, so the train's front wheels both come off," Derek explained showing the man what to do on the paper.

"Now comes the hard part, just as the engine is derailed a team of men have to throw their explosives into each carriage with a short fuse, about half a meter length, not very long to get away, but looking at the area opposite it will do. Once you have thrown the explosives leave at once and go home. Are there any questions?"

After a few comments Derek said he would show them how to set up the explosives, and gain some practise on the best way to throw them. He also told them how to booby trap roads. "On a road you can never be certain that the wheels of a vehicle will run over the explosive, if it doesn't someone else might, so one way is to plant your explosive where there are trees or other objects that you can put a thin cord across, suggest fishing line not easy to see when driving, tie the line to one object bring it to the explosive, wrap it around the detonator then around the other side object and back to the first about a meter off the ground, as soon as the line is broken, boom."

Derek went on to tell them of other methods before they left, saying to meet at the railway line at 0130hrs, which should give plenty of time to go over the plans again.

After a big bowl of broth, Derek and the others met at the railway siding near where they would derail the train, Derek went over and over what had to be done. The two brothers went along the track and started separating the line, the men that were going to throw the explosives went to their positions along the track.

"Once more," Derek said, "when the train starts to run off the track, light the fuse on your explosives and aim for the middle of each carriage, once you have thrown get away quick. Now we wait."

At 0308hrs the sound of the train could be heard, not far away. "Get into positions," said Derek.

The train slowed down as it got near the bend, everyone

was tense and ready, suddenly there was a loud grating noise as the engine began to topple over, followed by the carriages, the explosives were thrown well as the train fell into the side of the buildings. Everyone was running across the open ground towards the woods when there was a loud explosion followed by many others. "I think it worked," Bart said to Derek as they headed for the council yard.

All the next day the area was crawling with Germans, they were busy clearing and mending the track, fire engines were busy; the whole scene was one of total carnage.

"I'll give it two days and then I must get back, two days to go over other ways on how to sabotage," Derek told Bart and Renee.

CHAPTER 18

Admiral Webster studied all the information with mixed reaction.

"I suppose it's always good to disrupt the enemy, and getting rid of that new long range submarine was worth the raid."

Sergeant Myers had arrived back at Plymouth after being picked up by the Lysander aircraft.

"Quite a bit of damage: admin block, stores depot, sleeping quarters and mess hall, all destroyed. Plus some high ranking officers killed or in hospital, also a nice job on that train derailment, how would you feel about going back and operate with Bart and Renee?"

Admiral Webster asked Myers as he stood up and walked to the window. "Should we now move Lt. Carter elsewhere?"

134

"I would suggest to the Normandy coast, we could do with another agent there, keeping us informed of troop movements etc.," remarked General Long, who was part of the combined op's team working at Plymouth.

The admiral thought for a while. "Better we should have someone with experience then a new chap, I'll get a signal to him explaining where to go."

***

Marie found Richard standing looking at the damaged office block, that had been the administration offices. "A message for you from Plymouth, father received it, he's not sure if he got it right."

Richard read the note. "They want me to go to Caen in Normandy and meet with a Jean LaMar at the Hotel Stram."

"When will you be going?" Marie asked.

"Tomorrow." Richard thought for a while. "Why don't you come with me?"

Marie was undecided, she would like to go but worried about her father.

35

That evening while sitting talking Richard told Laurie, who said he thought it a good idea. "It will probably be safer for her as things are getting hard here at the moment road blocks everywhere, Germans always asking for papers. Us oldies can sit and wait, but you young ones make the most of what you have, we never know how long it will last."

Richard and Marie began packing a few things. "Don't take much it only draws attention, the radio we will have to put under our seat and hope for the best," Marie explained.

Laurie told them the Hotel Stram was only about 200 meters from the railway station, then wished them goodnight, saying breakfast at 0700hrs.

Richard and Marie talked for a while before going to bed. "Let's hope we are doing the right thing, I worry in case anything should go wrong and I've put you in danger," explained Richard.

"My choice. Now let's get to bed, early start in the morning," replied Marie.

Next morning Laurie had a good breakfast ready. "Where did you get this lovely ham from?" Richard asked.

"Never mind, friends among friends," he said. "Now a change of plans, I've arranged for you to travel with Maurice, he transports coal and he is going to Caen, so put on these old clothes and blacken your face, you should look the part," he said with a grin.

Just after nine Maurice pulled up outside, Richard and Marie had changed into old clothes and looked like they worked on the coal truck.

Maurice told them that if they got stopped, which is most likely, to act normal, say good day and let them search the truck. "I've got a space under the front bags of coal under the flooring for your stuff that should be OK. Now I suggest we get going, it's a long journey in this old truck."

It took all day to reach Caen, having been stopped twice. It was almost 7:30 p.m. when Maurice pulled into his coal yard, just off Caen's high street.

"You can wash and change in my house, I'm sure my wife will have something to eat. You can stay here for the night, that way you won't be out after curfew."

Maurice's wife Adelle made a bed up in a spare room. "This was our son's room, he is now in England with the free French," she explained to Marie.

"Thank you that is very kind," answered Marie.

The night was peaceful, after travelling all day they both slept heavily, only being woken by Adelle with coffee. "Breakfast in ten minutes, I hope you both slept well."

"Yes thank you, very well, and thank you for the coffee," said Marie waking Richard. "I think you had better have a shave if we are going to a hotel."

After a very welcome breakfast they thanked Maurice and Adelle for their hospitality.

***

Marie looked at the Hotel Stram. "Looks very impressive," she said as they headed towards the reception desk.

"Good morning," the receptionist said. "Papers."

"Good morning," replied Richard. "I'm looking for Jean LaMar."

"Could I ask who is asking?" said the receptionist looking at their papers.

"My name is Richard Cartier, and this is Marie Fern, I believe Mr LaMar is expecting us."

"Please make your way through that door and into the

office, LaMar will be right with you."

Making their way to the side of the reception desk and through the door they entered a large office which was full of boxes and cabinets, overall quite a mess.

The receptionist came in from another door. "Please sit down, I'm Jean LaMar, glad you made it safely," he remarked shaking hands. "Sorry about the mess, I've had to put everything from my store room in here; the Germans have taken over part of the hotel, including the store room."

"I'm not sure why I am here, but as long as I can help," Richard said watching LaMar pull out an envelope from between some books.

"This I will destroy after you have read it, then I think you will understand."

Richard read the letter. "I understand. When do I start?"

"This afternoon. Maybe in the meantime you could walk around Caen, get used to the streets? Be careful keep out of the cafés where you see lots of soldiers, go to the Café Rhoo in Rhoo Avenue, but be back by 1600hrs."

***

Richard and Marie began walking through the main shopping streets of Caen, looking at the shops that used to be busy, but now there was just a few people around. They were surprised of how many soldiers were about, walking from one café or bar to another.

"Look at that uniform, infantry. Those two over there are pilots, I must make a note of the different uniforms," Richard declared.

They found Rhoo Avenue, and soon found the café, making sure no Germans were about they entered: two elderly men sat in a corner, a middle aged woman was behind the counter.

"Madam Lou?" Marie asked.

"Yes can I help you?" she answered.

"Mr LaMar suggested we should talk to you," Richard said with a light smile.

"Take a seat over near those two gentlemen, I will bring some coffee."

Richard and Marie sat at the table next to the men, who were looking at Richard.

"Mr LaMar sent you, who is Mr LaMar?" one said.

"Mr LaMar, or Jean LaMar, is the owner of the Hotel Stram, we arrived yesterday from Brest."

"How did you get to Caen?" the other man said.

"We came with Maurice on his coal truck, his wife put us up for the night," said Marie.

Madam Lou came with the coffee. "Welcome to Caen Richard Cartier and Marie Fern, we were told you were coming, sorry about the questions but you understand we have to be careful."

"Quite," Richard replied. "I understand by the letter I read I am to gather as much information on troop movements, uniforms, etc. and what goes on around this area, and report it all to you Madam Lou."

Madam Lou and the other two gentlemen joined Richard at the table and opened a box of dominos. "Just in case any Germans come in," she said spreading them over the table.

One gentleman explained to Richard he must also note and report to Madam Lou all types of installations the Germans have along the coast, all messages were to go in and out go via Madam Lou. "I understand you have a new radio, you can use that as you usually do, it won't hurt if you and Madam both send messages, but keep her informed at all times, it's quite an undertaking. Germans are everywhere, just act normally, don't rush. If you think anyone is following you don't come here go to the town gardens, it's big and you should be able to lose anyone."

"Thank you all, I expect to be in touch soon," Richard said as he and Marie left the café Rhoo and headed back to the Hotel Stram.

CHAPTER 19

Sergeant Derek Myers was once again asked to go to France, this time at the request of the French resistance in Châlons, which was not far from the German border.

"There is a large ammunition factory just outside of Châlons, the French would like someone who knows explosives and also could monitor air strikes, it's a dangerous spot but the factory must be destroyed, it's not visible from the air so an accurate position is needed," Admiral Webster explained.

Sergeant Myers was given instructions of who he will be working with. "Your first contact will be Marco Torrie, he is of mixed blood: part French, part Spanish, but loyal to France. He will meet you at the landing site, the Lysander will take you all the way, if there are any problems, and it can't land you will bail out."

Derek asked if it would be best to bail out so the aircraft need not land.

Admiral Webster spread out a map of the area. "We would like the plane to land as we hope to bring back another agent that is in need of attention, that is who you will replace."

"When do I leave?" Derek asked.

"Tomorrow night should be OK, the weather looks like being overcast with a little rain, not good flying weather but ideal for the Lysander."

***

0240hrs in the morning; the Lysander pilot noticed the signal from the landing area. "Looks like it's OK to land so hold tight it could be bumpy."

The landing was indeed bumpy, as soon as the plane stopped six figures appeared, the changeover was very quick, Derek only saw the back of a man being helped into the Lysander which turned around and was in the air before the rest of the men approached, Derek introduced himself. "Is Marco Torrie here?"

"I'm Marco Torrie, pleased you made it safe, now we should leave here."

After about twenty minutes they arrived at a barn. "Stay here until 1030hrs when someone will come for you." Marco and the rest left Derek with some food and drink.

***

Derek was up and waiting when into the barn came a hearse, fully loaded with a coffin and some flowers. "Good morning I am Jean Claudel the local funeral director. You will please change into this suit, you are now part of the funeral trade, we are about to give you your first funeral."

Derek changed then got into the back of the hearse, which headed towards town.

"After the funeral we go back to my shop where you can stay, I have a small spare flat over the shop, which is also our HQ, the resistance meet there. We are glad you have come, we can do a lot of things, but some things are new to us, we are hoping you can show us. We know where the factory is, you will have to identify the major targets within the factory, there are also plenty other targets around this area so you will be busy. We don't do any sabotage work, as reprisals are always very heavy, observations and report only. Right let's get on with this funeral."

The days passed, Derek had seen the factory and met a lot of the resistance, they were very interested in what he showed them: how to get a position using a simple compass or a watch, how to direct aircraft onto targets, and plenty of other useful tips.

The day came when he was told a night raid on the factory was due, Marco and some friends together with Derek would go to the factory area and make a line on both sides of the factory using small flares, the bombers would bomb anything between the flares, once the raid was over the resistance should try and recover as many used flares as possible, Derek would then make a report on the damage.

That night they made for the factory, everyone knew what had to be done. "It's 0130hrs, light the flares," said Derek, "the bombers are due in two minutes."

Suddenly the whole place was ablaze, bombs were exploding all over the factory area, the resistance had moved back away from area, but still the ground shook. It seemed never ending: buildings were exploding, others were set alight and small explosives going off, then came the quiet, followed by the sound of fire tenders.

"Let's see if we can find any flares," Marco said heading back to the spot they had planted them, "don't want the Germans finding any."

Derek began making notes of what he could see, before they all went back to the funeral home to work out if it was a success.

"We are only missing four used flares, just hope they don't find them," Marco told Derek.

Two days later Admiral Webster received the report.

"Gentlemen, just received this signal from Châlons. *Target 80% destroyed, more targets around, will advise. Nice job, well done fly boys. D.M.*"

CHAPTER 20

Six months passed. Christmas had gone, which was a time of little joy, the soldiers must have been told to disrupt any celebrations; a bad time.

It was now into March, with its chill winds. Richard had been able to gather quite a lot of information on what was around the coast: what type of sea defensives, what type of guns, number of troops, all kind of information. This was passed to Madam Lou for forwarding to Plymouth.

Richard had been given a bicycle with a big basket on the front and back, and every morning he would deliver bread and rolls to the elderly on the outskirts of town. He became a familiar face, stopping at houses and an elderly hostel, he always had a pencil and note pad writing down next day's orders, and anything of interest he saw. All was working well.

Richard and Marie had just finished breakfast in the Hotel Stram. Marie had said she was going to help Madam Lou while Richard was doing his bread run.

"Good morning Mr Cartier, or should I say Lt. Richard Carter, Royal Navy?"

Richard looked up with a start; it was the young officer from Fécamp, Heinrich Mass.

"The last time I saw you, you were being picked up by an English MGB, I'm surprised to find you here. I still have the note you left, saying you killed Yvette Du'rio and her husband," Heinrich said sitting down at their table. "And who is this young lady?"

Richard noticed Jean LaMar talking to a porter, and looking towards him. "This is a young lady I met last night, we seem to hit it off. I like her very much. She knows nothing of my past, only as Richard Cartier - bread delivery man. Just let her go now, please."

"What am I to do with you? I love my country, but not who runs it, the sooner this war is over the better for us all. Now what are you doing in Caen? No good I expect."

"Nothing at the moment," Richard replied.

There was a commotion at the front door, six German

soldiers and two SS officers came marching in. "Papers please everyone!" shouted one, heading towards the table where Richard and Marie were. Heinrich Mass stood up and walked over to the soldier. "This lady is my guest for breakfast, be more polite."

The soldier stopped, looked at Heinrich then to a SS officer who was talking to Richard.

Heinrich turned to the SS officer saying, "I am Captain Heinrick Mass, internal affairs, and this gentleman is also with me, we are here on official business. Next time I would expect you to acknowledge a superior officer. We were just leaving as time is important."

The SS officer apologised for the misunderstanding as he gave Heinrich a salute, which Heinrich acknowledged. Outside Richard asked why he had done that. Heinrich replied that the SS didn't represent the main German people, and that they do more harm in Germany than anywhere. "I will leave you now, I hope we will not meet again while this futile war is still going," touching his cap Heinrich turned and walked away.

Marie watched him as he turned the corner. "Why can't they all be like that?" she said.

"I think we should get our belongings from the hotel and ask Jean LaMar where we could go as I'm now recognised in Caen."

***

"What was that all about?" LaMar asked as they went into his office. Richard explained all that had happened in Fécamp. "Is there any place else we could go?"

"Stay in your room, I'll be awhile," LaMar said as he put on his jacket, "I must go and see Madam Lou."

Three hours passed it was just getting dark before LaMar returned. "Tomorrow morning you can go to Arromanches, a small village on the coast with not very many Germans. A friend, Louis, will meet you, here is his address, don't get caught with it."

"Thank you for your hospitality Jean," Marie said giving Jean a peck on the cheek.

"You have both done enough in this area, we will carry on until France is free."

"How do we get there?" asked Richard.

"You will travel with a funeral party, we use them quite

often as the Germans mainly ignore funerals. Madam Lou has sent some suitable clothes. The vehicles will pass the hotel at 0900hrs, if you wait at the side entrance and watch they will stop for a short while as the deceased worked in the hotel, you get in the van at the back marked De'Chon family butcher."

CHAPTER 21

The following morning was going to be busy for Heinrich Mass, he had to organise a reception at the Hotel Stram for the area commandant and some VIPs, so he was up early. Road blocks were being put at junctions leading to the hotel.

Heinrich had told Jean LaMar at 0600hrs what was happening and expected full cooperation from his staff, the party should arrive about 1030hrs, the street would be closed as soldiers lined the route from 0900hrs.

LaMar explained at 0900hrs a funeral party would pass the hotel, stop for one minute then head for Arromanches.

"If it's on time I will let it pass, otherwise an alternative route must be used," replied Heinrich.

Richard and Marie had breakfast bought to their room and were told what was happening.

"You must get ready early and wait in the laundry room, the door opens to the side street just a little way from where the funeral will pass when it slows to a crawl get in the van quickly."

Heinrich had instructed the guards at the barrier to let the funeral party through.

Heinrich stood at the hotel entrance as the funeral party slowed Heinrich noticed two figures emerge from the side of the hotel and get into the butcher's van.

Turning back into the hotel he called for LaMar. "That was well done, please don't make my life any more difficult, let's hope Mr Carter has a safe journey. Now let's get on with the matters in hand."

***

It took nearly three hours to get to Arromanches: they had two check points, and one road block to get through. The van driver stopped near the address Richard had shown him. "It is just around the corner, you should be alright here, never too many Germans about."

Richard thanked the driver and funeral director, then

154

went looking for No7 Rue Burn.

"Good afternoon can I help you?" the man said.

"Are you Louis?" Richard asked.

"Yes, you are Richard Cartier, and this must be Marie Fern, please come in," he said bringing them into a cosy warm room which had a nice fire going.

They were soon talking about Madam Lou and Jean LaMar. "How is the old dog, still finding time to help others? He is a good man. My wife is shopping at the moment, then we can eat, my wife is also called Marie."

Marie came in with some shopping. "Hello I'll get us all some dinner, maybe the young lady would like to help me while the men talk?"

"I'd love to," Marie said going into the kitchen.

Louis put some more logs on the fire. "I have a package for you, which will give you all the information you will need. We don't get many Germans here, there are some fortifications along the coast, but it's not too difficult to get about. Things have been quiet, maybe a few signs of troop movements, which is what the English would like you to do: troop movements, fortifications, any type of Panza units, things like that, and contact times and frequencies."

Louis's wife Marie said dinner was ready; a thick vegetable stew, which was very welcome.

***

Meanwhile back in Caen, Captain Heinrich Mass had welcomed the area commandant and other VIPs.

"Well done Heinrich, you seem to have things in hand."

"Yes sir, apart from a young SS officer, must keep an eye on him, the meeting should go alright."

The meeting that was taking place in the hotel was behind closed doors. Heinrich was standing by the door when the SS officer approached.

"I wish to go into the meeting, I am head of security in this area."

"The meeting is nothing to do with security, its private military matters, I'm not allowed," Heinrich explained.

The look on the SS officers face told it all.

An hour passed before Heinrich was called into the meeting. "Captain Mass we have discussed the proposal and agree that for the sake of Germany and its people we must try and eliminate the source, and then try and negotiate a ceasefire, you say you have an idea that may work?"

Heinrich looked at the six high ranking officers. "Yes I think I know an Englishman who would fit the bill."

"Can he be trusted with such a job?" asked one.

"I'm sure he can, and would probably jump at the chance. He killed his own mother who betrayed his father to the SS in Fécamp."

The idea was agreed, the meeting ended with all parties saying farewell, and agreeing to meet again once the job had been done.

Outside the hotel Heinrich was organising the transport for the VIPs, when the young SS officer asked how the meeting went. He wanted to know if there were any changes he should be aware of for security reasons.

"If there is you will certainly be the first to know," replied Heinrich.

***

1030hrs the next day Heinrich knocked on the door of Louis's house.

Marie opened the door. "Good morning, is Richard Carter in please?" said the man in the brown suit with a German style hat.

Panic set in, Louis and Richard pulled out their revolvers,

"There is no need for that, no one is with me, and no one knows I am here," Heinrich remarked taking off his hat.

"Why have you come, and how did you find me?" Richard asked.

"You have been followed by my aid since I saw you in Caen, he is very good, a German ex-policeman."

"You are taking a risk, you probably want leave here alive," Louis said as he asked Heinrich to come in.

"I have a proposal for you, if you take it I can protect you and your friends," Heinrich told Richard and Louis of the meeting and what was proposed. "If an Englishman could do the job it would make us that are left to pick up the pieces easier, we could then go into talks with the allies without the witch hunt of who was responsible."

"So what would you want me to do?" Richard asked as Marie came into the room. "The road is clear, he is on his own."

"Hello again," Heinrich said to Marie with a short bow.

"Hitler is expected in Caen in two weeks time to look at the barrack area, they wish to enlarge it for more troops, you can guess why. I can get you into a position with which you can hide after without being found. The area will be crowded with troops, so I intend to hide you in the back of my staff car, it will be among other vehicles in a holding area waiting to collect the soldiers from the streets. I have two English 303 rifles, one for you the other my aid will place just in the woods outside Caen. As soon as you have done your deed get under the back seat I will come straight away, every vehicle will be on the move looking for the shooter, I will then drop you somewhere safe."

"And if things go wrong?" asked Richard.

"You will be on your own and we will try again some other time, there are a lot of top men who wish this to happen. I will let you know when, if you do not wish to do this don't worry I will walk away and this meeting never took place, if you will do it I must know tomorrow. I am staying at the local Hotel Remour, but only for one night."

CHAPTER 22

Squadron Leader Archie Wells, walked into the Op's room
of Mosquito squadron 47. "Good afternoon gentlemen,
tonight we are going to bomb the coastal batteries and
army barracks along the coast at Arromanches. It's a raid
designed to disrupt their build up of coastal defences. Each
crew has its targets: red leader will attack the guns along
the coast line, green leader will target the army barracks
and vehicle depot. This is a drawing of the gun
emplacements along the coast." He pointed to the wall
board." The army barracks are about two miles in land,"
once again pointing to the board, "we will take off at
2130hrs, low flying once over France. Good luck
gentlemen."

***

Meanwhile Richard told Marie and Louis he must go out and try and make sense of what Heinrich Mass had said. "I need to clear my mind, to work out what to do."

Richard was standing by an old seafront café near to where a big coastal gun was pointing out to sea just as the sirens went off. He thought *good our bombers going over to somewhere.*

Richard was too far from Louis's house when the first bomb fell destroying a gun next to where he was. He took shelter in the passage between the café and toilet block.

Richard never heard the bomb that destroyed both the café and toilet block.

EPILOGUE

April 1946.

Heinrich Mass walked into the British HQ in Berlin.

"Could I speak to someone about a missing English agent please?"

The military policeman escorted Heinrich into the office of General Thornton.

"How can I help you?" the General asked.

Heinrich told the story of what had happened to Richard Carter, and his association with him.

"So you say this man killed his mother? I'll get on to the Admiralty, they can verify all this. What happened to this Marie Fern?"

"She went back to St. Brieuc, to her father's house, I think she continued with the resistance."

They continued talking for another two hours, covering Heinrich's affairs in everything.

"Well thank you very much, every little bit helps to trace him, we start in the morning," General Thornton said, walking to the door with Heinrich and watched as he walked along the street.

Heinrick looked up at the clear blue sky. *A nice day,* he thought, *now let's get busy rebuilding Germany, maybe one day we will all be friends.*

Sergeant Derek Myers continued with the resistance until the end of the war, making a name for himself; remembered to this day.

END

Other titles in The Carter Family Saga

Tea, Traitor and an MTB

Lightning Source UK Ltd.
Milton Keynes UK
UKOW04f0256121113

220873UK00001B/3/P